Escape from Crimea

A Collection of Short Stories

Svet DiNahum

Červená Barva Press
Somerville, Massachusetts

Červená Barva Press
P.O. Box 440357
W. Somerville, MA 02144-3222

www.cervenabarvapress.com

Bookstore: www.thelostbookshelf.com

Photo credit: Natalia Zhurminskaya

Cover Art: Images courtesy of Wikimedia Commons

Cover Design: William J. Kelle

ISBN: 978-1-950063-41-3

Library of Congress Control Number: 2020947369

Dedicated in memory of my friend, translator, and poet Valentin Krustev (1949 - 2016), a true friend of America and American literature, translator of Irwin Shaw and many American classics

Dedicated to the American – Bulgarian literary partnership and friendship

Special thanks to all translators and editors from Bulgaria and USA for their unique help with this book: Valentin Krustev (1949 - 2016), T.M. De Vos, Matthew Brown, Angela Rodel, Vessislava Savova

TABLE OF CONTENTS

"There are too many books I haven't read, too many places I haven't seen, too many memories I haven't kept long enough."
— Irwin Shaw

Escape from Crimea

Escape from Crimea

BASED ON ACTUAL EVENTS

The sun descends in a red flame over the Dobrudzha Plains, over the Free West, warming the sunflowers for a few final moments. At my back lies the Black Sea, which carried me here from Crimea, saving me from tyranny, allowing me freedom from the inconceivable audacity of a dictatorship. But the memory of my suffering lives on, burning just like that fiery sphere before me. Scenes from my life before and after blend together in my mind. Here, in the present, I see before me thousands of wind turbines, clustered across the great plains, spun by the breeze. Each rotation, each whirl of a blade, is a punctuated, eloquent whisper into the ether: "Why? Why? Why?" I turn east to the Black Sea and look across the dark water toward the horizon. Somewhere there is my Crimea.

I am Tanya, a Ukrainian from Sevastopol. I was a chemical engineer in a large production plant for artificial fertilizers. The plant ran on enormous quantities of natural gas, which came from Russia at twice the price of that in Europe.

Until 2014 I lived fairly well, although my salary was modest. I am 29 years old, not yet married. I come from a small village near Lviv. My parents live there still, as do my sister and her husband. I shared an apartment owned by the plant with my colleague Masha, who had managed to leave Kazakhstan and the Nazarbayev regime and find quiet refuge in Ukraine. She was a nuclear engineer.

I am no nationalist, and I was not particularly interested in politics. But I expected our leaders to be decent and honest people. Science was my hobby and I dreamt of pursuing my doctorate in chemistry at Sevastopol State University.

When ordinary Ukrainians resisted our corrupt president Yanukovych and his criminal faction, we accomplished something wonderful. Things changed. They may have shot us in the Maidan in Kiev, and we may have been beaten by the Berkut special forces, but in the end we were victorious. Yanukovych was removed from power and fled to Moscow – the source of his orders for a long time anyway. Freedom, hope and the possibility of a new, independent life were all within reach. We were on a path toward Europe, toward the European Union. We had freed ourselves from the shackles of Putin and the war of imperial dissimulation that he waged on our country. At least, that is what happened for most Ukrainians. But not for us in Crimea.

In March of 2014 a referendum was called in Crimea about joining Russia. This was against the Ukrainian Constitution, but for all intents and purposes Crimea had already been occupied by Russian special forces, paramilitary units, secret Russian militias, armed bands and commandos. They had installed a commandant, a governor, a militia commander. On orders from the Kremlin, they announced and scheduled the referendum.

On the day of the referendum they gathered us all in the courtyard of the plant. Heavily armed men appeared, bearing no military insignia, led by a tall, strong, middle-aged man who called himself Chesnyakov. We later learned that he was a colonel in the Russian special forces and a veteran of the Soviet-Afghan War of the 1980's.

"Think very carefully about your vote tomorrow!" barked Chesnyakov loudly and commandingly. "Remember that Crimea is and always will be Russian! Anyone who votes no may have to worry about where they're going to work and how they're going to live."

We stood in somber silence. Our grey-haired director, a man of dignity, dared not say a word and stood in the back of the courtyard.

When we went to vote, all of the voting stations were surrounded by Crimea's new, pro-Russian militia. There were tanks, AK-47s, machineguns, other guns, many soldiers and officers.

At the school where I was assigned to vote, young Ukrainian boys were demonstrating peacefully against Crimea joining Russia. Suddenly they were attacked by paramilitary units, along with gangsters and former Berkut forces. These beat up some of the boys and threw them like dead dogs in a big dumpster. They left others lying bloody on the pavement. Others they loaded nearly lifeless into military trucks of some sort.

I voted against. Most of my colleagues voted against. But somehow when they announced the results that evening, it turned out that 93% of Crimea had voted to join Russia. And that was the beginning of my own personal hell.

Just a week after this so-called "referendum," which had been carried out with Kalashnikovs pointed at the citizens, our old director was replaced, and they began firing the Ukrainians at the plant.

We held a strike in front of the plant. We held up posters: "Stop firing Ukrainians!" "Energy independence from Russia!" "Think about food for our families!"

My roommate Masha and I, along with around ten colleagues, held up a huge sign:

STOP THE OCCUPATION OF CRIMEA!

Suddenly two large commando units and civilian paramilitary formations came out of nowhere. They came at us with clubs and sticks. They dragged people along the ground and kicked them in the head.

They grabbed our unit head, Ivanchuk, and pulled him in front of us to make an example of him. Colonel Chesnyakov stepped over. He had now been officially put in charge of the Crimea militia.

"I warned you!" Chesnyakov shouted. "Who do you

think you are? Well? Disgusting Bandera revolutionaries! Knuckleheads! Imbecile rustic peasants! I told you, Crimea is ours! You bunch of trash!"

Chesnyakov pulled out a pistol and shot behind Ivanchuk's head. The man thought he was dying, and he crumpled to the ground, terrified. We sighed in relief when we saw that he was alright. But then Chesnyakov, grabbing him with one strong fist, lifted him by the collar out of the dust, put the muzzle of his gun to the back of Ivanchuk's head, and pulled the trigger. It was a horrifying sight – blood and brains sprayed out in our direction and the people in front got splattered. I watched as Ivanchuk writhed on the ground and then convulsed before finally going still. It was the first time I had seen a person die. I turned around and vomited. All around, women and men were throwing up, cursing, pleading, crying and screaming.

Chesnyakov stood in front of us and laughed.

"Any more protests, you rats? Well? Who wants to join Ivanchuk?"

We trembled in silence.

The commandos arrested twelve of our union organizers, loaded them into armored jeeps, and disappeared, led by Chesnyakov.

I didn't sleep a wink that night. I kept picturing poor Ivanchuk's shattered head. Chesnyakov's ugly face kept popping out at me, yelling, "I'll send you to the bottom of the Black Sea for the fish to gnaw the skin off your bones!" Old fears and traumas kept me awake as well. I recalled my first job as a junior engineer, at a natural gas metering station on the Russia-Ukraine border. My role was to monitor the gas transit, to take samples to track the quality and quantity. During the night shifts I noticed that Russia was putting less gas through, and with a composition of lower quality than had been agreed to. Ukraine was being defrauded while paying exorbitant rates. I recorded the data diligently in the record. I didn't know or suspect then that the head of the transit station was a Moscow man. He destroyed the records, and to get back at me he came to me when I was on night duty, pressed me against the control panel and groped me roughly. I pushed him away and slapped him, ran from the station in the dark of night, and walked six kilometers in the December cold to get to my hostel. I was lucky not to be attacked by the nasty street dogs that often inhabited this unpopulated border area.

In the morning, my face puffy and eyes bloodshot after a sleepless night with not a minute of rest, I went to work, in total shock from the horror and violence that were still fresh in my mind. My colleagues were in the same state: defeated, despondent, confused, depressed. They started calling us into the new director's office one by one. My turn arrived in just an hour.

I went into the plant director's office, quivering and terrified.

He was seated behind his enormous desk, a remnant of times in the USSR when the plant was called Leonid Brezhnev. A large portrait of Vladimir Putin hung over his head.

Grinning maliciously, the director did not invite me to sit, but left me standing by the door. He fixed his eyes on me and murmured:

"Effective immediately, consider your employment terminated. And as the apartment is plant property, you and Masha must be out by tonight."

"But I … That would leave me out on the street… Are there grounds for my termination?"

"There are. Incompetence, and serving as a bad influence on the work environment. That's all. Have your things out of the apartment by eight o'clock tonight and leave the key with the porter. Dismissed."

I turned away, grabbed the doorknob, started to open the door. Then I turned again to face the director, and whispered:

"Criminals!"

He just laughed even more deviously and reached for the phone to have his secretary call in the next rebel identified for termination. He glanced up at me with revulsion and spoke with a scowl, in a low and emphatic voice, almost a hiss:

"Get the hell out of here, Bandera trash."

In the late afternoon Masha and I gathered our modest belongings, vacated the apartment, left the keys and walked out into the street, out of work and homeless. She was planning to go to her brother's place in Kiev.

We went to a club by the sea, a bar and coffee shop called Admiral, to say our goodbyes. We had been roommates and good friends. We had participated together in the strike, and together they fired us.

The rough waves hitting the shore below moaned like an unfairly wounded giant, rising to exact revenge against a mob of infidels.

At just that moment Masha and I realized that what we had known as our country was coming to an end.

We each ordered coffee, and then suddenly sensed an unseen threat. We glanced around timidly at the tables nearby and were horrified to see colonel Chesnyakov.

Sitting like a king in a booth that was off limits to regular customers, a $2000 bottle of Louis XIII cognac lying empty on the table, Chesnyakov demanded a cigar. He was drunk and his mood was dark. The waiters behaved like servants, bowing obsequiously as they presented two large wooden boxes for his inspection. He chose an enormous Cuban cigar, and the head waiter made to light the cigar with an ordinary lighter. As a result, the wretched and foolish servant received a whack across the face, and if he hadn't jumped aside in time he would have received a kick from Chesnyakov as well. The bartender saw what had happened and ran over with a long wooden cigar match.

And he placed it on the table without a word. The colonel struck the match and took obvious pleasure in turning the cigar while drawing the flame along its length. He repeated this process with another match. He went through a third. And then another, and one more after that. Finally, he lit the cigar, nodded and leaned back.

His telephone rang.

"*Zdravstvui*, Sergei!" Chesnyakov's commando voice thundered throughout the bar.

Then he listened carefully to the explanations on the other end, and ordered:

"Yes, *horosho*, buy the refinery in Genoa! Transfer two billion from the office in Lausanne! I'll deal with Berlusconi afterwards, we're meeting next Monday!"

Clearly the caller then asked a stupid question, because Chesnyakov scowled and responded sharply:

"It's none of your business where! Do what I say and report back! That's all! Until further contact! And if you come up short, remember Mayakovski! You remember his last words, don't you, before he 'killed himself?' 'Comrades, don't shoot!' Over and out!"

At that moment a customer in the next booth, angry at the noise, shouted furiously:

"Hey, caveman, what world are you living in, man? Why can't you let people enjoy their drinks in peace?"

Chesnyakov didn't even turn around. He simply lifted his left hand, bent his fingers to a right angle, hid his thumb beneath them, and with a slight sideways gesture pointed this simulated blade toward the left side of his neck.

Four elite commandos jumped up from a table in the corner, expertly grabbed the customer, and dragged him outside, all the while beating him on the head. They threw him onto the dock, kicked him for a while, and then threw him into the breakwater. (The next day the newspapers said he had gotten drunk and drowned.)

Even this bloody event that was so suited to his taste failed to brighten the evil Chesnyakov and distract him from his gloomy, dark, drunken dejection.

Every second he was puffing on his expensive Cuban cigar, he was a man of power from Moscow. He started talking to the empty space in front of him:

"People came to power who wanted to establish a unified order. Made of iron, of steel. I was created and produced by these very same people, those who helm the Kremlin, with the ship in the hands of a great, new Admiral. You joined up with the doomed and rejected, with traitors to Mother Russia, with the liberals! This is what you get, you imbeciles! Eh, you lived well for ten years or so under that troll Yeltsin, yes! You stole. You robbed. You sold our country to the Americans! But now your end is coming. I'll destroy you all!"

Ironically, he himself was a high-level official in a huge oil conglomerate, a whole empire. He was in the top elite of Russia and dined only with the top elite. Even that hotel across from us was his – just another pearl in his crown, just like that, for variety.

Chesnyakov mumbled to himself:

"Grandpa Aleksei, veteran of Sevastopol… Ah!"

Then he looked up and sang in a loud voice, raspy and frightening:

We set off a few of us strapping young men

Behind every fusillade ten of us sailors.

The nymphs of the sea, they wordlessly beckoned,

But we were protected by our St. Andrei!

"I dedicate this to the sea!" cried Chesnyakov. "Yes, to the Black Sea! The Song of Admiral Ushakov!"

Then he turned to his commandos, most of whom were also drunk, and to the bartender and the waiters, and commanded:

"Sing with me boys! Don't be cowards!"

A discordant sound rose over the surf , raspy and dark, like a chorus of drunken sailors, or of pirates:

Standing before us the Sultan himself,

And blacker than death stood his blackamoors too.

But our hearts were eager to hasten to glory,

And we were protected by our St. Andrei.

"The vile Americans are to blame for everything!" Shouted Chesnyakov. "And their underhanded agent, the traitor Gorbachev! I will never forgive him, I, veteran of the battle of Kabul! Who abandons whom? The older sister abandons the younger? And then the young one despises her? Absurd! No, Ukraine is the younger sister and she will be ours, ours, ours! Crimea is ours already! Glory to the heroes of Sevastopol!"

Suddenly Chesnyakov's blurred glance fell on Masha and me. The hair rose from our skin.

"Oh, you, Bandera whores! The ones who were protesting at the chemical plant, right? I know you, yes! Now you will dance! Take off your clothes immediately. I want you naked!

Chesnyakov's commandos pulled us up from our table, one pointed his machine gun in our direction, others beat us, ripped our clothes, stripped us completely naked and forced us to perform a belly dance before Chesnyakov's table. I remembered how my Russian supervisor had groped me at night at that gas metering station on the border. This humiliation now was many times worse, increasing my psychological trauma threefold. They toyed with us, laughing like idiots, and the drunken chorus continued to shout wildly:

Our numbers increased, we teemed from the sea —
Souls without fear, seasoned by blood —
Volley after volley, we felt quickened on the swells,
And from up on the mast: faith from our St. Andrei!

Chesnyakov snapped his fingers and they brought him another bottle. He grabbed it and filled his squat glass to the rim with cognac.

"Bottoms up, Colonel!" He toasted to himself.

Then he downed another. And another one after that.

"To honor!" He yelled frantically. "A volley for Colonel Chesnyakov! A many who was and always will be true to mother Russia! To the officer of honor, Pavel Chesnyakov! To the fact that if necessary he will die with his head held high, understood and forgiven! To Colonel Chesnyakov, who heeded the voice of the Admiral! The voice of the true President! A salute to the President!"

He emptied the entire magazine of his Kalashnikov into the ceiling. Slivers of silver sextants fell from above.

Then he turned to us:

"Now get out of here, Ukrainian bitches! Go disappear off the face of the earth! Protest against me, will you?! Call us occupiers, the owners of Crimea!? You'd better go hide on the moon, because if you're anywhere in Ukraine I'll hunt you down! My trusted agents are everywhere! I've looked into your whole story. Yours too, Masha. I'll find you with your brother in Kiev, and you, Tanya, I'll bring you in for the pleasure of my boys. That's right, I'll drag you out of that village of yours near Lviv, where your mother and father are, and your sister and her husband, and I'll bring you in as the company plaything, you dirty Bandera rag. Get out, Ukrainian slime! Bandera whores, both of you, out!"

The commandos threw us out on the street, naked. We were scared to death, and ashamed. We hid in the dark corners, away from the light of the streetlamps. We took shelter in the quiet yard of a house near the pier, hiding among some dark bushes. We cried and sobbed and held on to each other. There was no longer a place for us in Crimea or Ukraine, Chesnyakov had warned us, and he knew the names and addresses of our relatives.

A lamp in the house went on unexpectedly. The door opened and we saw an elderly couple with a flashlight. They shone it on us. When he saw we were naked, the man turned away. The woman called to us:

"Come here my dears. We heard what happened. Some neighbors were at the Admiral club, and they told us that Chesnyakov had done terrible things to two young women. That must be you. Come. Come in. Don't be afraid."

She showed us to the bathroom. We bathed, and she gave us clean clothes.

Then they set the table and invited us to eat. Their name was Savchenko. They were pensioners.

"What are you going to do now?" He asked me.

"I don't know," I answered. "I want to go to Bulgaria.

"Why Bulgaria?" asked Mrs. Savchenko.

"Because the only option I can think of is that I have a cousin in a small town in the northern part of the Bulgarian Black Sea. I think it's called Shabla."

"Have you been there?" Mr. Savchenko chimed in.

"No. I went to Bulgaria once for vacation, but that was in a resort, Golden Sands, a completely different place, and it was long ago.

"Then how will you track down your cousin? Do you know her family name?"

"Her name is Natalia. Natalia Harchenko. But she married a Bulgarian, a sailor, and she probably changed her name. I can ask people about Natalia the Ukrainian, she's a piano teacher as far as I know, and it's a small town, so someone will surely know her. Hopefully she can take me in at first. Besides, Bulgaria is in NATO and EU now. Kremlin has no power over it whatsoever, it is not like before, thank God... I will be safe there, far from Chesnyakov's clutch."

My roommate Masha was quiet, afraid. Mr. Savchenko gave her a look of concern and critical resignation, like a parent worried whether his child will be able to handle what lies in store. He sighed, and then looked at me again.

"And how do you plan to get there?"

"I don't know. By bus?"

"Hmm. The border between Crimea and Ukraine is closed. And the new border police, all Russians now, might have orders to report to Chesnyakov when they see your passport. Don't count on him forgetting just because he was drunk. He is a dangerous Moscow dog who's brought tears to many a mother.

"Well, what should I do then? I asked sadly.

"I can help you," answered Savchenko. "Since my pension doesn't go very far, I make some extra money as a fisherman. I have a small motorboat. If the sea is calm I can get us to the northern shore of Bulgaria. I have a GPS, so we can find Shabla. As far as I've heard from other fishermen, there's a lighthouse there, and a fishing pier and a quay where I can moor the boat. I can leave you there and come back. If the weather is good it'll take me ten or fifteen hours one way. But… It will cost money. For fuel, but not just that. The risk is huge, if the Russian coast guard catches us. They'd confiscate my boat, they'd fine me, and they'd even throw me in jail for human trafficking… It's really dangerous, you know…

"How much?" I asked excitedly, seeing a chance to escape to freedom.

"Well… Around three thousand dollars…"

I was quiet for a second. I had two thousand dollars in the bank. I told him honestly:

"I have only two thousand. That's all I have. As God is my witness."

Mr. Savchenko exhaled quietly, thought for a moment, and then nodded and said:

"Fine. What else can I do? You're one of us, Ukrainian, ill-treated, afraid, tormented. I'll help you. Bring me the money tomorrow. Right now there's a storm, but the forecast calls for it to end within two days, and then they're expecting at least two days of tranquil seas. That will be enough for me to get there, leave you, and return. We'll go the first night possible after the storm.

Masha sat there quietly, worried.

"Will you come with me? I asked her. Then I realized she might not have any money.

"Mr. Savchenko, could you take both of us for the two thousand that I have?" I looked pleadingly at my host.

"I could," answered Savchenko simply. "It's true that…"

"I have some money saved, that isn't the problem!" Masha broke in quickly and nervously. "I'm afraid! I don't want to fall into the hands of those guys from the border police! I don't want them to drug me! I don't want to dance naked! I don't want them to grope me, or they could even rape me!"

"Alright, alright, take it easy," I patted her shoulder. "What will you do then?"

"I'll take a risk and try to get to my brother's in Kiev by bus. Whatever happens, I have to make it there! I can't stay here! I got out of Kazakhstan before, away from that impudent despot Nazarbayev. I found quiet refuge in Crimea and now Putin's come along with his gangsters! There's no rest for a regular person! No peace or dignity! And no freedom at all! Only dictators!"

The next day, Masha said goodbye to me and the Savchenko family. I saw her off at the bus station. She boarded a bus for Kiev. I watched through tears as she looked for a seat among the other passengers. She took a seat by the window and smiled at me. I wondered what her fate would be, whether she would make it. My heart ached, for her and for me too. The bus pulled out slowly. She started crying too, she couldn't help it. She blew me kisses and waved through the glass.

"Farewell," I read on her lips.

"See you soon, Masha!" I yelled from the platform of the Sevastopol bus station.

I went to the bank and withdrew my savings, and that night I gave the money to Mr. Savchenko.

"We leave tomorrow night," he said, and he handed me back a fifty dollar bill. "Buy the things you'll need for the trip – food, especially canned things and crackers, take plenty of water, at least one change of warm clothes, batteries, medicine, cigarettes and a bucket. Mine is very dirty."

On the day when we were to depart, I went to the market and bought everything I needed, including the bucket that Savchenko told me about, although I did not understand why he needed it. But I could not find cigarettes anywhere – there had been a shortage since the Russians occupied the peninsula. I went to a guy on the black market who always had a secret supply. In recent weeks he was the only one who had hard-to-find items, though always at twice the price.

He gave me a carton of cigarettes. He was quiet and focused. I pulled out the money. But he shook his head and refused to take it.

"Your money's no good with me today," he said carefully. "Put it away, you'll need it. And don't even think about coming back – for now there's no way back. Your friend Masha they arrested at the border. Who knows what will happen with her. So get out of here as fast as you can."

I felt a deep pain. Poor Masha. Sorrow filled my eyes with tears. Then suddenly I realized something and my heart filled with fear.

"But how… How do you know these things?" I asked timidly.

"Smugglers know everything," he replied darkly. "Come on, quickly, get out of here. May God protect you."

When night fell we climbed into Savchenko's motorboat and quietly moved away from the fishing pier. As we started to leave the inlet, we saw powerful lights in the sea – Savchenko explained that these were Russian missile boats, torpedo boats, destroyers, cruisers, frigates, and gunboats, and there were submarines too. Helicopters were circling in the sky, and I could hear the whine of airplane engines.

"They brought in an aircraft carrier, too, the bastards," said Savchenko. Look, their fighter planes are always taking off, and others are landing. They won't leave our Ukraine alone! They took Crimea from us. May they rot in hell!"

We had put some distance between us and the lights, and I was praying to make it out when out of nowhere a strong spotlight shone on us from the darkness and we heard a rough male voice through some kind of bullhorn:

"Stop! Coast Guard!"

"Shit!" Savchenko cursed. "Quick, come over here."

Savchenko hid me in a barrel, and on top of the barrel he threw some old fishing nets, ropes and some kind of greasy rags that smelled like oil. The barrel was at the dark end of the deck, in the corner, and through a slit between the boards I could watch what was happening.

The Russian cutter pulled up alongside our boat, and boat hooks and ropes landed. Four strong, well-built men jumped aboard the fishing boat, landing deftly near Savchenko. One of them leaned on the barrel. I could smell smoke from a lit cigarette.

"Where are you going this time of night, old man Savchenko?" Asked the cutter captain slyly.

"I have nets out for flounder. I'm going to check the catch."

"Is that right, in the middle of the night?"

"Well you know our tricks. It's warmer now."

"Sure, it's warmer, but don't try to bamboozle us. It's barely the end of March and you're looking for flounder, for god's sake?"

"Oh, I got mixed up. I'm an old man and sometimes I don't make any sense. It's goby that I'm out for."

"Even for goby it's too early."

"It isn't too early. There's goby out there. Just three days ago, before the storm, Kovalchuk pulled out a couple of nets and…"

"Enough, enough!" The coast guard captain cut him off sharply. "Enough nonsense! It's just sea snail out here now, and only during daylight, and we know you're not out for snails. You're not here for fish. I'm guessing it's contraband cigarettes. So let's have a little taste!"

Savchenko sighed, pulled out a hundred dollar bill. He handed it to the captain, who scowled and erupted angrily at the old man:

"Are you fooling around with us? You want to sleep behind bars tonight? Get it together, man!"

Savchenko sighed even more deeply, pulled out another hundred, handed it over, and said:

"Boys, I don't have any more, that's all."

"Fine." The captain pocketed the money, with a dissatisfied look. "I'll let you go this time, but don't let it become a habit to be so stingy. You know very well this isn't enough, and next time it's not going to work, remember that! But if you pay regularly and well, you won't have any problems with us. Now let's get out of here!"

The captain hopped back into the cutter, and his men followed. They gunned the engine and disappeared quickly into the darkness. The motorboat was left rocking in the wake of the fast-moving vessel.

I breathed a heavy sigh of relief. I heard Savchenko saying softly:

"Best to stay a little longer in the barrel until we get out into neutral waters. You never know who else might turn up! Bandits!"

After about half an hour he was kind enough to pull me out of the barrel. I had to pee really badly and I asked where the toilet was. Savchenko laughed and handed me the bucket that I had purchased.

"Here's your toilet. You can use it at that end there, behind those casks. Don't worry, I can't see anything from this side. I have another bucket for myself, but I'm ashamed at how dirty it is. That's why I asked you to buy your own bucket, which will be clean at least at first."

We laughed for the first time in three days.

The sea was smooth and calm. There were clouds here and there in the sky but it was mostly clear. You could see the half moon and many stars.

The motor hummed along evenly and quietly. Savchenko gave me some blankets and I slept in the cockpit. He stayed at the helm, smoking one cigarette after another, pouring coffee from a huge thermos, adding a bit of rum from time to time.

At dawn Savchenko nudged me in the shoulder to wake me up.

"Come take a look at something beautiful!"

I woke up right away. At first I had trouble figuring out where I was. I was afraid and started to yell.

"Relax, relax my girl! You're among friends! There's nothing to be afraid of anymore!"

I gathered my wits, calmed down, and looked in the direction indicated by Savchenko's callused hand.

I saw a few large dolphins jumping and diving close to the boat, giving off their special sound. This made me happy.

"You see, we made some sea friends," said Savchenko with a smile.

An hour later we docked at the fishing pier beyond the Shabla lighthouse, in Bulgaria.

The sun was rising over the sea to the east.

Savchenko helped me out of the boat and placed my bags on the pier.

"I hope you find a home here!" He said. "Good luck!"

He turned toward the boat, started to board, but then turned around and sighed, coming back toward me. He put his hand into some hidden inside pocket and handed me one thousand five hundred dollars:

"I don't have the heart to leave you alone in a foreign land without a cent to your name. You can't start a new life without any money at all."

"But you said… I mean …" I started, emotional and confused.

"I know, I know, this time I'll do it with no profit," Savchenko smiled. "What I have left will more or less cover the fuel. Be happy!"

And then he jumped quickly into his boat, turned on the engine and started back.

After that things turned out well for me. I found my cousin and she and her husband took me in for a while. They helped me find a job as a lab technician in a local cable factory. People in town are good and kind. I rented a place on my own, a small, old house near the sea. The yard is full of fig trees and pomegranate trees. Grapevines hang above them, and Nohan grapes fill with sweet juice. Swallows gather on the wires, the sea shimmers and sparkles, and they're harvesting sunflowers in the fields. The fishing boats leave the inlet in the early hours and return full at dusk. My small, immaculate rooms are furnished with old pieces, covered with lace. In the air there is a scent of Bulgarian herbs – *chubritza*, Queen Anne's lace, pennyroyal, spearmint, lemon balm, thyme, lavender, linden. And the scent of village life, of a simple life, of gentle forgetting under the stars. Life somehow goes on.

That is my story.

And at the end of each day I come back here, by the Black Sea. The rosy sky at sunset sorrowfully covers the scars of the advancing blue-grey. But there are wondrous icicles there, the work of a tender mermaid who has unexpectedly acquired artful wings. And the piles of God's creation – the canvass sail of silent destiny – are once again worthy tonight of the last flight of the sea eagle.

As in Sevastopol, here too the sea sometimes moans like an unfairly wounded giant, rising to exact revenge against a mob of infidels. Revenge against whom? I am not interested in revenge. I want only peace and freedom. I found them on this side of the Black Sea. It is hard for me to believe that I suffered so much only because I wanted to be free. But so it is with tyrants. It's in their blood.

Deep inside I maintain hope that my Crimea will recover from dictatorship, free from the shackles of a foreign burden and oppression, and will see a new life without Chesnyakovs and Putins. I dream of returning one day to embrace my mother, my father and my sister. We never had a chance to say goodbye.

Until then I will always look to the Black Sea, across the dark water, and my heart will fill with longing for my lost motherland, I will want to forget my suffering, my wounds and humiliations. I hope not for a barren wilderness but for a new spring, not for poison, but for restorative waters.

I will never give up hope, even at night when I whisper to the
east through bitter tears:
     "Farewell, my Crimea!"

Zoran

BASED UPON A TRUE STORY

Dedicated to the 20th anniversary of the Srebrenica massacre in Bosnia, and to peace and human dignity.

On a warm, sunny June day, Zoran sat, playing chess for keeps at an outdoor café at the edge of Central Park. He was winning pennies from the keen-eyed old men who had come to spend their Saturday outdoors. He was a psychology student at NYU, and he was among the best basketball players for the Violets.

The year was 1995, summer term was just starting, and the war in Bosnia and Hercegovina was roiling. Zoran was Serbian and convinced that the Americans had started everything in Yugoslavia by supporting the Muslims.

Birds lighted on the trash cans and backs of benches, and children threw them candies and crumbs of bread. The whole park glowed in the sunlight. A gentle breeze came, and the leaves rolled a little to show everyone their brightness.

On the lawn, towering above the sunbathers, stood Schiller's bust, as if to remind them of his words: "Beauty will save the world."

A man in a gray suit, with expensive platinum glasses over unflinching steel-gray eyes, approached Zoran's table with dignity. He looked about fifty. "Mr. Zoran Ristich?"

Zoran held his rook aloft, trying to look nonchalant. Had someone died back home? He thought of his brother, Branko, who had enlisted. "Flesh and blood. What can I do for you?" He set the rook down decisively. "Check."

His opponent, a kind man in a grey felt hat, gave him a quick nod and stood up, pushing his coins to Zoran's side of the table. The stranger moved in, taking the vacant seat.

"My name is Militarevich." He put out his hand, and Zoran extended his own. "I am from Belgrade, just like you. A Colonel."

"I see." So he was here to recruit him. "I don't know how much good I'd be to the Serbian National Army. I'm just a student."

Militarevich waved his hand as though chasing an impertinent fly. "Zoran, I would like to acquaint you with my proposal." He paused, then bored into Zoran's face with his metallic grey eyes. "I am sure you are a patriot."

"Of course." He kept a big Serbian flag tacked to his wall over his bed, and wore a hat with the patch of the Republika Srpska coat of arms while he played Frisbee in the park. Fighting was for older guys. Like Branko. *Tougher*, he amended, remembering that he was only two years younger.

"You know we fight the Muslims. And you know America is supporting them. It's our duty to the motherland."

Zoran flicked at his knight with his thumbnail. "I have to think about it." That was what he said when someone stopped him in the street, asking for money or a signature on a petition. "My brother is in the Army," he offered, so that Militarevich would know his family wasn't a bunch of slackers.

He nodded, curtly. "We know. He must be your hero."

"He is." Branko had always been the brave one, the one who backed up his words with action.

"Keep in mind, the motherland is calling. If we lose Serbia, we lose everything. If we lose our dignity, we lose our souls. And all shame will be upon us." Colonel Militarevich opened his briefcase and pulled out a heavy volume, titled in English: *Serbia: The Superior Nation of the Balkans.* "Read this." It was easy to see how he had risen to the rank of colonel. There was no mistaking his authority.

Zoran nodded, half lifting his hand to salute. "I will, Colonel."

"Call me Dusan." The Colonel smiled, just another middle-aged man now, someone you'd see at the *kafana* or pass on the street. "My card is in this book. Call me when you're ready."

Branko hadn't needed a book, or time to think. "I will, Colonel," Zoran repeated, meeting his eyes.

The Colonel snapped his briefcase shut and stood up. "Today is Vidovdan. Five centuries ago King Lazar led our soldiers against the Turks in the Battle of Kosovo. The dark powers creep over our fatherland again, supported by these bastards here." He made a gesture that included all of the bastards in the café and in the park. "If we betray our land, King Lazar will curse us from heaven." He pushed in his chair. "Don't wait too long."

*

Zoran survived in his dorm thanks to the frequent parties he threw. The loneliness of the city could not be overcome by studying or watching TV, or by eating the discount pork chops he cooked in his small kitchen. The usual company always met at his place: the two Bulgarian sisters; Takoshi from Japan, who lived downstairs; Peter the anthropologist; Michael from the Upper West Side; Roman the Latvian Jew; Misha Shestakov the Russian; Steve the Republican; Katherine the artist from Manchester—the original, not the one in Missouri, or in Georgia, not even the one in New Hampshire—Kyle the polisci major; two or three other random guys who were always up for a beer; and, of course, Joe the Commando. But his two best friends in America were Takoshi and Michael.

The enormous moon pushed in through the window. Inside, the company was gathered over drinks, indulging their nostalgia for the '80s with old AC/DC songs. Zoran was imitating the late Bon Scott, and the girls were laughing.

"Where's Takoshi?" somebody asked.

Zoran looked around. "I'll call him."

But he didn't answer his phone.

"He's got nowhere to go. Maybe he's asleep, dreaming of samurais," Roman said.

"Could he be with his girlfriend? Or just some girl?" Katherine asked, impish.

"Maybe in virtual reality," Steve the Republican quipped.

Somebody turned the stereo on, blasting the Grateful Dead. Zoran looked around. There was plenty of vodka and beer. Misha Shestakov had dragged over a gallon jar of pickled cucumbers and was arguing with Peter the anthropologist about the origin of the recipe: Russian, Indian, or Jewish.

Roman burst in, pale and sweating and disheveled.

"Dude, you need a beer," Steve said, mocking as usual.

"Let me get a cigarette." Roman passed his hand over his eyes, rubbing them hard.

The CD ended. In the silence, everyone examined Roman.

Roman exhaled the cigarette smoke and began to cough. "Look out the window."

They looked out. An ambulance and four police cars had piled up, blocking the street. Bursts of red and blue light revolved in the windowpane. They watched, wordless, as a stretcher with a covered body was carried out and shoved into the ambulance.

"It's Takoshi," Roman said tonelessly. "He jumped out the window."

"But why?" everyone kept asking.

"It's just that Takoshi…" Zoran trailed off. "He didn't feel comfortable here." They had discussed it often. Zoran understood.

Everyone was confused and talking over each other. Only Joe the Commando sat in a corner, motionless and quiet. He radiated a quiet, almost mercenary, wisdom.

Zoran needed to get away. He perceived the evening not just as one awful night, but as an endless succession of brutal currents in a deep, narrow stream. To fight the current, to run away, would be salvation. But how?

He glanced at the book from Colonel Militarevich. In the dim light, he opened to a random page blazoned with King Lazar's curse, in lurid italics:

> *Whoever is a Serb and of Serb birth,*
> *And of Serb blood and heritage,*
> *And comes not to the Battle of Kosovo,*
> *May he never have the progeny his heart desires,*
> *Neither son nor daughter!*
> *May nothing grow that his hand sows,*
> *Neither dark wine nor white wheat!*
> *And let him be cursed from all ages to all ages!*

The back of his neck prickled, and he turned to see that Joe the Commando had followed him.

"Joe? You were in the military, right?"

"Special forces. The Green Berets."

"Where?"

"El Salvador. And my father is Mexican. How's that for irony?"

"What were you doing? Cutting off communists' heads?"

"Pretty much. Until I almost became one of them. When you go somewhere and kill people, at some point you start sympathizing with them. That's what violence does to you."

Zoran nodded. "They're calling me up now. For Serbia."

"Free advice from a Green Beret: Don't go. It's all lies."

"I feel like I want to. If I stay, I'll be a betrayer." He decided not to mention King Lazar's curse. Joe would think that was a lie, too.

"That's ridiculous." Joe's sneer made him look ominous, like a gargoyle, in the low lamplight. "You go and serve some bastard politicians who will disappear after awhile. Only you might disappear first. What for? Don't put patriotism before your own life."

"I got a letter from my mom. My brother is in a military hospital. She says fighting the Muslims drove him crazy. Who's going to pay them back?"

Joe laughed—a low, joyless bark "You can never pay them back. You'll just lose the life you have." He gestured around the room, at the computer on Zoran's desk, the textbooks haphazardly stacked on the dresser, the narrow unmade bed.

"If this is so great, why do people commit suicide?" Embarrassed by his volume, Zoran cleared his throat.

Joe smiled bitterly. "I don't know. But if you kill someone, you'll never get your dignity back. You'll be ruined." He walked towards the window, his back to Zoran. "I should know. I've lost count of how many I killed."

Zoran watched him silently.

Joe jerked the cord, and the blinds clattered onto the sill. "Remember what I told you, when you go off and serve the devil."

Zoran called the number tucked away inside the book. "Mr. Militarevich? I mean, Colonel?"

"Yes, Zoran."

"I'm ready."

"Good. I'll send your ticket today. I am proud of you. May God's will be with us. Fight for heavenly Serbia, part of God's New Promised Land! We are the people of Heaven!"

Zoran listened as the Colonel went on, writing down his instructions and making agreeable noises as he tried to put Joe's words out of his mind: *Ridiculous. Dignity. Serve the devil.*

Zoran argued passionately with Michael, who had come to see him off at JFK, until the last minute. "I have to defend my motherland. Those American bastards are occupying my country!"

"Man, I'm an American bastard and I'm telling you: this is a waste."

But Zoran wasn't listening anymore. He raised the book so that Michael could see the title and gave him a mock salute. "Take care, man." *I am following the destiny of a true patriot*, he told himself as he entered the gate.

*

Zoran arrived at Belgrade Airport in July. His first impression was that everything was very small and grey. After his years in America, he had forgotten almost everything: how people looked, how the streets looked. The memory of his favorite places was thin and pale. He saw so many Yugo cars at the airport lot; now they looked to him like children's toys.

He visited his mother and father. His sister, Militsa, hugged him and cried: "Zoran, what are you doing? This is a terrible waste of your wonderful life in America!" His mother cried; his father stood silent and depressed.

"Father," said Zoran, "I am doing the right thing. For the Motherland! For the sacred national cause! For Christianity!"

"No, son. This has nothing to do with what I believe in. I thought all nations in Yugoslavia would live together in peace. What happens now is the dirty work of the politicians and the superpowers behind them."

Zoran and Militsa visited the Military Hospital in Belgrade to see Branko. It was surrounded by iron fencing and barbed wire. Inside was total misery: at least twelve soldiers packed in each room, dirty bathrooms, lousy food, and chaos.

One soldier wept on the floor against a wall. Another marched in the corridor, saluting unseen officers and calling, "Yes, sir! Aye aye, sir! Enemy approaching! Boom! Tra-ta-ta-ta-ta!" Yet another soldier was hiding from a nuclear blast only he could see. In the corridor, a soldier was running and crying out, "Let me out of here! Let me fight! Let me serve!" A doctor with a full syringe ran after him. A group of soldiers in the corner sang a military tune in falsetto while one beat an imaginary drum in accompaniment.

Suddenly, the steel door swung open, and four orderlies carried a stretcher holding a tall, strong soldier who thrashed and struggled. As he contorted his face and gnashed his teeth, Zoran had a flash of recognition. He turned to Militsa.

"Branko," she whispered, almost soundlessly.

They watched as the orderlies overturned the stretcher and dumped him onto an empty bed. They started slapping him in the face, screaming at him to calm down. The pillow turned red.

Attendants brought a straitjacket and managed to wrestle it onto Branko. A doctor ran in, pushing a cart holding a square metered box and two long cords. They forced a rubber stick between Branko's gnashing teeth and turned the dial all the way up. Branko screamed like hell. All of the patients joined in his howls. Soldiers cried, jumped on their beds, and smashed their few belongings.

Zoran and Militsa stood on the sidelines, silent and shocked. Zoran thought of Militarevich, cool and sane and composed. *He must be your hero.* Across the room, Branko's back arched sharply, propelled by a surge.

*

After a few more tense days at home, Zoran hitchhiked to Srebrenica by night. He got on the road and saw a sign that read: "Srebrenica: 120 kilometers." *About 75 miles,* thought Zoran. He walked along. Vehicles passed him, mainly trucks. He stuck out his thumb when the headlights flicked over his solitary figure, but nobody stopped.

Suddenly, a figure popped out from the bushes. Zoran jumped.

It was an older soldier, uniform almost torn apart. "Relax. I am a fugitive," he reassured Zoran. "I am running away from hell."

"Who are you?" asked Zoran.

"I am not going to tell you my name. I am escaping from a military penitentiary, from a Punishment Company. Where are you going?"

"Srebrenica."

"Are you from there?"

"No. I am from Belgrade. But yesterday I came from New York."

The older man started laughing. "Oh, yeah? And I came from Mars." He stopped abrupty and looked around. "Enough talking. Time is not our friend. Let's keep walking and try to stop a truck. I need to get to Srebrenica, too."

As they walked on the side of the starlit road, forest enclosing them on each side, the soldier said: "It is not possible that only good exists in this world. Evil is an equal opposing force. Evil is real. Actually, it is stronger. Rules the world. Sometimes I think there can't be so much evil in the world. But bad won't go away just because you turn a blind eye. You, my unexpected companion, are still young and should remember this."

Zoran barely had time to reflect on this speech before a truck approached. They waved their hands, and the truck driver slowed, then stopped. They got in.

Zoran had an uneasy feeling. He saw himself as if from outside. Something told him that he would remember the whole scene for the rest of his life. He gazed out at the now-empty, dark, and narrow road, overhung with century-old beeches. The beam of the truck's headlights bored through the thick, horrifying darkness, an artificial light in a world without sun.

*

In Srebrenica, Zoran saw tanks, cannons, army squads, and the heavy military trucks that transported the bodies of dead Muslims. Serbian soldiers shoveled dirt onto them from the edges of a mass grave. Zoran swallowed hard, thinking of his last conversation with Joe: *You can never pay them back.* Or maybe you could, but it cost you something, too.

"Zoran!" someone called.

Zoran turned around and recognized an old classmate from Belgrade. He was taller now, of course, and leaner, with a sharp face that could have been engineered for the military. There was little sign of the boy who was always last to catch on, last to laugh at a joke, last even at physical culture. "Dragan? What are you doing here?"

"Protecting the Fatherland," Dragan replied with enthusiasm. "We're cleansing the whole area—no Muslims, no enemies, just us Serbs!"

Zoran peered at Dragan, trying to reconcile the dull boy he had alternately teased and pitied with the charged, wiry soldier in front of him.

"We used mortars to destroy the villages. We are amateurs, though—we didn't know how to figure the range, so we just fired them, checked where the blast was, and moved backward or forward. We were running up and down the hill like crazy: total clowns!" Dragan laughed at the memory, then squared his shoulders again. "Still, we managed to kick some ass. Now we're burying eight thousand Bosnians in a single grave.

Zoran looked back at the row of soldiers, still hunkered down over their shovels. A fine silt rose over them like fog.

"Well, we kind of killed them." Dragan's old matter-of-factness hadn't entirely abandoned him. "What else? Now it's time to celebrate."

The old schoolmates wandered around Srebrenica and went into a tavern called The Powder Keg. A live band played wild, brutal tchalga. The singer's bleating seemed to comment on the mass madness around her. Zoran and Dragan took seats at a long table amid a crowd of soldiers from the Serb National Army, para-military gangs, mobsters, and women determined to sell to the highest bidder. Covering the walls were lithographs from the old kingdom, war totems, military flags, coats of arms and logos for the Republika, for the Army—Serbian and Yugoslav—and portraits of General Mladic, Radovan Karadzic, and Slobodan Milosevic.

"We are the powder keg of Europe!" people from the crowd were shouting.

"Down with England!"

"Down with NATO!"

"Down with USA!" A colonel drew out his pistol and fired into the ceiling.

"Down with Moslems!"

"Viva Serbia!"

"Viva Radovan Karadzic!"

"Viva General Mladic!"

"Long live Milosevic!" A trio of military gangsters fired their Kalashnikovs into the turf in front of the pub.

"King Lazar, pray to God for us! King Lazar, curse our enemies! Curse us if we ever betray you!"

Zoran wondered if he was at the wrong place, in the wrong era. Everyone and everything around him looked ruthless, narrow, and ignorant. All of his late-night debates with Takoshi and Michael about ideas, ethics, what people had a right to expect from life, what they owed each other—what did they matter, now that he'd been thrown in hell? Why hadn't he stayed in New York? Nothing here had any connection with rightness or justice—anything he and Takoshi had, over beers and instant noodles, declared was worth dying for. It didn't even feel like the motherland, as Colonel Militarevich had said. This fiery, howling pit didn't belong to the Serbia of his childhood: the Serbia of the village, with its pecking chickens and pushy babas.

"Feeling out of place?" Drunk already, Dragan was shouting in Zoran's ear. "Don't worry! Tomorrow you'll become a real Serb when you shoot your first Muslim trash!"

Zoran smiled wanly and looked away quickly, worrying the label on his bottle of Niska. "Unless America changed you! You're not in New York anymore—this is the powder keg of Europe!" He gestured slackly at the sign and tossed back the astringent dregs of his rakia.

Zoran felt all this Balkan bacchanalia surrounding him. As a child, he hadn't understood the Balkan madness, Balkan pain, Balkan, Balkan tragedy, Balkan deadlock, and Balkan doom. He wasn't tough enough to be a man here, in this harsh, savage, place; America had softened him. He expected comfort. Order. Peace. He expected education, talent, hard work, and honesty to pay off. Not here, in this kingdom of aggression and brutality.

Did I just throw away every opportunity I ever had? Zoran thought of his abandoned dorm room, the textbooks he had left out on the street with the trash. Even his secondhand futon looked, in hindsight, like a luxury. He pictured himself, happy and oblivious in his room, surrounded by Serbian kitsch. Involuntarily, he thought of Branko, gagging and convulsing as the doctor dialed up the current. Of his parents, and poor Militsa, unarmed and defenseless in the village.

Every young person thinks that his own tragedy is unique, and uniquely impossible to solve: it is a variety of youthful arrogance. It is also how the young fall victim to fanaticism. It is inevitable to be changed by living somewhere else. And in Zoran's case, the change was for good.

*

The next morning, Zoran reported to the camp, dirty and cotton-mouthed and still in his street clothes. In the midst of the crush, he could see that the other soldiers were dressed in new uniforms. The official emblem of the Army of Republika Srpska stood in stark relief against the dark fabric: a white, two-headed eagle crowned with gold.

The soldiers lined up. In the back, Zoran did his best to line up his toes with theirs so that his dusty, unwashed self wouldn't stand out. A stout, grey major with fanatical eyes—a lunkhead, his clumsy, self-satisfied bearing nothing like

Colonel Militarevich's straight-spined dignity—mounted the stage and settled himself behind the podium, next to the Socialist Party Secretary.

The soldiers around Zoran quieted down as if they had been snuffed.

The major looked out at the ranks, and thundered: "He who does not have anything here—" he pointed at his head, "has to have a lot here." He pointed at his biceps, and Zoran thought guiltily of Branko, his considerable muscles directed now by an empty shell of a mind.

"She who does not have much here," the major continued, pointing at his chest and puffing it out to comical effect, "has to compensate with this here." He pointed at his crotch. "This is the whole philosophy of life. Understand?"

The soldiers laughed. Zoran pushed air out through his own mouth, too.

The major frowned. "I know why you are laughing! You think the military is a joke. In fact, it is a factory for making knights. *Our* factory, which will make us the winners of all of the battles against the imperialist NATO armies!"

The soldiers wiped away their remaining smirks.

"Are you scared?"

They straightened up, squaring their shoulders a little more, puffing out their chests behind their insignias.

"Chickens? What do I see here? Only chickens! Ha!" His eyes traveled up and down the rows. The soldiers shifted uncomfortably, each sure the major was looking at him.

"From this point forward, the weak will be cast out. Only the strong survive!"

The men cheered. Zoran did his best to look as if he were joining in.

The major began barking, almost joyful now. "Company, attention! Lieutenant, close the ranks! Forward march! Toward victory!" He turned to a tall, morose-looking man. "Sergeant, call the tune! Give the pitch!"

The sergeant began an old Serbian military anthem in a fine, metallic baritone. Soldiers joined him, tentative at first, then roaring as they marched out of the compound and toward the front line.

Zoran stood aside, next to an old Soviet tank, and watched them leave. He couldn't just march out behind them in his NYU t-shirt and jeans. His sneakers were too clean, his clothes too visibly new, even in their unwashed state.

"Zoran Ristich!" An officer loped up to him smartly, checking his roll. "You are the volunteer from New York?"

"Yes, sir." Zoran tried to look enthusiastic, ready to fight, like the young men around him. Like Dragan. Or Branko, when he had first joined up.

"Barrack Eleven. You'll find your uniform and your weapon. Back here in two hours sharp."

"Yes, sir." Zoran saluted, clumsily, and waited for the officer to take his leave before he started toward the barracks. They were a mile back in the direction he had come from, near Srebrenica.

The officer hadn't warned him that that mile was called Snipers' Alley. Neither had Dragan. No one had.

Zoran was walking in the middle of the road, in plain sight, when a single, silent, faraway shot struck his heart. His body fell on the dusty ground. Because of his baseball cap, his new sneakers, his NYU t-shirt with its purple-colored mascot, the Serbian snipers had thought they were aiming at the American enemy.

Casablanca Memories

The diamond clock at Sotheby's in New York City marks 10 a.m. And the electronic calendar nearby shows the date: October 10th, 2010.

"So many tens", thinks Alexis Weissenberg.

"Let us start the auction", says a lady from Sotheby's. "In the beginning, let me share with you that we are especially honored to have Mr. Alexis Weissenberg with us this morning. Let us all congratulate the greatest piano player of all times. Welcome at Sotheby's, Mr. Weissenberg!"

People applause him warmly. He stands up, gently bows to the public. He is 81.

The lady continues: "Today Turner Classic Movies puts up for auction some film memorabilia. We will start with the piano featured in the movie Casablanca. I hope you all remember it. This is the piano played in Rick's Café Américain. And Rick, of course, was the unforgettable Humphrey Bogart. So, this piano has a value which surpasses the material side of life many times. It carries so many memories and it is emotionally attached to the heart of every one of us. The piano in Casablanca…."

*

The silver clock on the wall at Vladigerov's house in the Jewish Quarter in Sofia strikes three. It is 1936. Pancho Vladigerov, the great composer, gives him piano lessons for free.

"Tenderness, tenderness, tenderness", says Vladigerov. "Only the tender hand placates the piano. The piano rejects cruel men."

Little Alexis leaves Vladigerov's house after the lesson. From the street he hears the composer talking to his neighbors David and Angel in the yard:

"The free world owes the poor kid a piano lesson."

*

1937. His first public performance in Sofia, Bulgaria. The audience is astonished by the talent of the small poor Jewish kid. Tremendous applause rocks the concert hall. He looks at his mother among the public. He sees her tears. Tears of joy, after so much suffering.

*

"SCHNELL! SCHNELL! SCHNELL!", German officers thunder at the skinny Jewish men carrying stones, iron rails, moving sand, cinder, scoria, and gravel.

It is 1941 and Bulgaria is ruled by the Nazis. Alexis and his mother are imprisoned in a German makeshift concentration camp. Most of their neighbors from the Jewish Quarter are here too.

Alexis plays Schubert on his accordion. One of the German guards listens very carefully and nods his head to show he is enjoying the performance.

In the middle of the night the same German guard secretly takes Alexis and his mother out of the concentration camp. He leads them to the train station. An owl calls in the dark from the gloomy military towers.

The rail station clock strikes midnight and at that very moment Alexis hears a long whistle and straight away he sees in the murky distance dim lights through a puff of steam.

Orient Express approaches the station and stops on its way to Istanbul. If they reach Turkey, they will be free.

"Hurry! Get on the train!", whispers the German. Then he shows his ID and sharply says something to the train guard.

Alexis and his mother run to the train. Alexis stumbles over the first footboard, but his mother quickly grabs him by the hand and pulls him up, into the carriage which is now their safe house. Locomotive lets off steam, Orient Express slowly starts moving. The German guard throws the accordion to Alex through the window and shouts:

"Good luck!"

*

1946. Julliard School. The great Artur Schnabel takes the class to a cinema in New York City. And they all watch *Casablanca*. Alexis is particularly intrigued when he sees the scene with the Bulgarian roulette player, Jan Brandel, and his wife Annina, in Rick's Café Américain.

"We come from Bulgaria. Oh, things are very bad there, Monsieur. A devil has the people by the throat. So, Jan and I, we, we do not want our children to grow up in such a country.",

Annina talks to Humphrey Bogart.

"Oh, but if you knew what it means to us to leave Europe, to get to America!"

And Humphrey Bogart makes a miracle. He winks to the croupier. The croupier makes some secret trick and Jan from Bulgaria wins a huge amount of money. Now he and his wife will be able to pay Captain Renault, the Prefect of Police in Casablanca, for exit visas, and to buy their tickets to America. Tickets to freedom.

Annina is so happy and thankful, she runs up to Humphrey Bogart and hugs him.

*

1947. Philadelphia City Hall tower clocks strike eleven at night. His performance of Rachmaninoff's Piano Concerto No. 3 has been brilliant. Alexis wins Leventritt Competition. Cassiopeia is right above Delaware. And the Universe sends him congrats for his success.

*

1957. Ducks are floating on the lake. Children are throwing them crumbs of bread and candies. The whole park is glowing in red. The tree leaves roll a little to show everyone their brightness, outlined distinctly in the transparent air.

On the lawn above the lake, on the still green grass, Schiller Memorial stands. In a semicircle behind it, charming tree crowns, fascinated, continue to tremble in red, orange, yellow and purple, reminding the passersby Schiller's words:

"Beauty will save the world!"

And suddenly he feels some kind of rare fatigue. He is exhausted by so many performances, by the concert halls, even by the public interest. He needs a long break.

He takes the subway to Cloisters to see his favorite tapestry – The Unicorn In Captivity.

And, without expecting it himself, he talks to the ushers – a lady and a gentleman:

"When I feel the living image speak to me, I say to myself, 'this is one of my musical paintings,' and that's that. Madam, I have truly been educated by these living images, and I can only tell you what they told me: *"Art is above cognition thereof."* And the more time I am in their presence, the more truths come like this, right into my head, and that, Madam, is the beauty of it!'

"Haven't you ever suddenly felt that you don't know anything, sir? That you don't know even the tiniest bit about the world, and that what you have considered your own knowledge is somewhat strange, foisted upon you, and, what is most important, counterfeit?"

"Before… Before the Purity was. Of yore. Before we were Springs. Before we were grass, trees, bushes, leaves, saps. Before there was a truth.

I am alone against the Entity. Certainly it must be so. According to the Substance, maybe. I do not know – but I am setting for searching the spring which I was said about it was an abstraction."

Before actually going out, he halts, turns to the Unicorn, stares at it. His eyes become moist and he says quietly: "I will, nevertheless, spend the night here, with you. What a merry feast it will be, won't it?! Nobody can ever break our spiritual connection. You are in my heart. Your art has changed me forever."

Then he starts towards the stairs.

Ushers remain for a little while longer, watching through the large windows to see in which direction the strange visitor is headed, just in case he tries to return. It is already past five. The sun is set behind the Hudson, and the park outside is sinking into glimmering twilight. The strange man is striding straight ahead, without looking around. Once he passes the Maple Leaf restaurant, there is no doubt that he is leaving. Now he is ambling along the lane where old Russian immigrants like to stroll on Sundays, under two large, bare trees, where suddenly, startled by something unseen, two owls flow past, one after another. And this picture remains, becomes imprinted on the consciousness of the watchers, because it seems to be somehow living, somehow talking to itself, and telling an unbelievable, yet perfectly real, painfully real story of the great talent in a need for a long respite.

*

1966. Delacorte Clock sings "*As Time Goes By*" with Sam's voice from *Casablanca*:

You must remember this,

A kiss is just a kiss,

A sigh is just a sigh,

The fundamental things apply,

As time goes by.

He opens an envelope he has received in the morning. He finds a ring, a letter, and a poem.

"Dear Alexis,

This is the ring of your father. I found it in your house after you and your mother left Bulgaria. I was cleaning the house and I found your writing on the wall:

"We left, my mother and I, without my father, with a small bag, a large cardboard box, a few sandwiches, an imaginary piano which appeared every time I closed my eyes, and an old accordion given a few years back as a birthday gift by a rich aunt."

Alexis, I found this poem along with the ring. It looks like your father wrote it. I want you to have it now. Alexis, I am proud of you. You should start playing again. For the world. And for all of us who love you.

Your Auntie,

Rosa"

He looks at the old ring. It is made of white gold, with a big black diamond on the top. He takes the paper sheet yellow with age and reads the poem:

The Immigrant Ring

The pain of Ellis Island breathes in me.
Across the common reverie of thousands of moans.

Across the dangerous cold ocean.
Across arms stretched out for farewell.

From high up in the sky I finally spread out
my wings over Manhattan.

Machines march; they plant souls to be called for,
and administer through me Holy Communion to shapes.

America, you are my favorite child.
I have sheltered in you millions of wretched creatures.

The pain of Ellis Island breathes in me.
America, kiss me now in parting.

The pain of Ellis Island breathes in me.
The old clothes rotted off in Europe.

The tempered wisdom was born from me.
And I laid it like a new icon over the North.

Around me resound salutes
Forgiving the rotten day of slums.

The pain of Ellis Island breathes in me.
America, my child, don't feel ashamed of us—the
nonmodern.

We built up the Canal and moved the Mountain, didn't we?
We shot one another in dark cross-streets, didn't we?

America, remember how we loved you

Lying sleepless in nightmarish hovels.

The pain of Ellis Island breathes in me.
And that's the trance about which they lie today sonorously.

The pain of Ellis Island breathes in us.
And that's the ring about which they make up plays today.

*

1966. Conciergerie Clock strikes nine in the morning. Paris meets him with clear skies, blue transparent air, brownish chestnuts, silver poplars, and tender aspens along the streets, holy-oaks, sycamores, yellowish maples and elms, thinned out by copper-beeches in the parks. His recital is scheduled for the same night. His first concert in 9 years. He feels full of life and talent again. He is ready for the public. He senses he is back. Incomparable feeling. Perhaps the letter from Auntie Rosa made a miracle... Just like Humphrey Bogart made a miracle for the poor Jan from Bulgaria.

*

1979. He is in Sofia for a concert. He is now world famous and the authorities in Communist Bulgaria cannot do anything else but to cringe before him.
He walks into Drouzhba Movie Theater. A big sign says:

Today's Special Retro Film Show: CASABLANCA.
"How can I help you, Comrade?", asks the lady at the box office.
"I want a single ticket to Casablanca", replies Weissenberg.
"A ticket to freedom."
"Okay", she smiles and hands him a ticket which looks like a cheap candy wrapper.

He watches the same scene with the young and attractive Bulgarian refugee couple, Jan and Annina Brandel, in Rick's Café Américain:

"We come from Bulgaria. Oh, things are very bad there, Monsieur. A devil has the people by the throat. So, Jan and I, we, we do not want our children to grow up in such a country.",
Annina Brandel talks to Humphrey Bogart.
"Oh, but if you knew what it means to us to leave Europe, to get to America!"

The crowd at the movie theater becomes exalted. People make direct association with the totalitarian situation in Bulgaria at that time. They laugh, they clap, they clump, they cry out:
"Yes, it is terrible in Bulgaria now!"
"Yes, we do not want our children to grow up here!"
"Yes, we want to escape to America too!"
"Viva America!"
"Viva Humphrey Bogart!"
"Viva Casablanca!"

*

"I have the pleasure to announce that we have a winner for the Casablanca piano. Mr. Weissenberg's bid is the highest one. Congratulations, Mr. Weissenberg!", auctioneer says.
One last applause from the people in the hall.

And he walks out of Sotheby's.

A crowd of journalists surrounds him at the exit.
"Mr. Weissenberg! Mr. Weissenberg! Mr. Weissenberg!", they call him to stop.
He smiles and continues walking.

"Mr. Weissenberg, what are you going to do with the piano from such a famous movie?", journalists ask him one after another.

He stops and tells them:

"I am going to donate it to the kids in the country I was born in – Bulgaria."

"Why?", a reporter asks him.

He smiles again and reminiscences overwhelm him. He closes his eyes for a while and he remembers so many things at once. Now, in the Fall of his life, he recollects his Springs, his Summers, and even his Winters. He opens his eyes and they become moist. He looks at the sky, he looks at Manhattan around him, he sighs a long sigh, and replies:

"Because the free world owes the poor kid a piano lesson. Only the tender hand placates the piano. This is what my Casablanca memories taught me."

Lona from Central Park

Late every afternoon, Lona would go to her little corner of our world. Resigned and shy, pensive, somehow sad, she would play in Central Park, setting an open violin case in front of her – for listeners, for passersby, for tourists.

She loved Vivaldi most of all. With his winter, spring, summer and fall, she, too, changed the seasons along with Central Park, year after year.

She had picked out a little corner close to the Schiller monument. And she was always repeating his words to herself: "Beauty will save the world."

Unfortunately, teenage rappers would often set up shop nearby, raising a racket and strangely enough, most passersby preferred to stop and listen to the rappers and toss down a few cents or a dollar there, and not by Lona.

The Mad Reciter was regularly strolling about nearby. He knew whole poems, novels, films, and plays by heart and would shout them out amidst the trees and the colorful groups of people coming here every day from all countries, from the whole world. The fountains chimed in, soothing his pain.

Today, too, the Reciter did not miss making his rounds of the park. He had glassy eyes and always and only looked straight ahead. Lately he had been stuck on Kafka. Now he went by, his arms spread wide open, loudly, frenetically repeating a single line from the "Hunger Artist": "the world was cheating him of his reward!"

This was a sign to Lona that she could now go.

She packed up her violin and headed towards the West Side.

She walked along the Hudson and stopped on the pier. There was a summer outdoor cinema. Free. They were showing an old film, "Cape Fear." She caught precisely the scene in which De Niro has slashed the nanny, and Nick Nolte slips and falls in a puddle of blood, then slips again and is floundering around, covered in blood. Some primitive guys in the audience started getting into the scene and yelling: "Yeah, yeah! Right on! Come on!" Clearly they found the horrifying image energizing. Lona shrugged, shook her head and left.

Further down the pier there was dancing. Retro-dances. A band was playing some mix of jazz, Charleston, rock n' roll and foxtrot. Dancing couples from at least three generations. A friendly looking young man invited Lona to dance and they whirled around amidst the others. Little multi-colored lights lit up the dance floor, sparkling ships sailed along the river, Manhattan glowed next to them. It was fun. Lona calmed down. Comforted, she took the subway home to her tiny apartment in Brooklyn.

*

The Fourth of July came around.

On her way to Central Park, Lona stopped by to see the fireworks. The preparations were mind-boggling. Thousands of people were scurrying from every direction, hauling blankets, bags of sandwiches, coolers full of drinks, grills, dishes, children, dogs and flags. Most of the police keeping order were in a cheery mood. Helicopters circled vigilantly above. Patrol cutters shuttled up and down the Hudson River, rigged out even with machine guns for the fight against terrorism. Paper American flags were being sold for two dollars. Later the price fell to one dollar.

Lona went to her corner of Central Park and started to play.

And only now did she notice the incredible uproar in the meadow across the way. A crowd of people, cameras, reporters, spotlights, lasers and a huge screen. With Britney Spears on it.

They had put Britney Spears in a porta-pottie filled with… with what toilets are filled with. They lifted up the toilet with a gigantic crane, high in the sky. Everyone started counting down: Five, four, three, two, one… And at the same time from the direction of the Hudson the fireworks for Independence Day started thundering. The noises mixed into one single wild and licentious choir, from dark to frenetic, the rumbling of the crowd, the thundering of the fireworks, the screeching of the fuses, Britney's crescendo towards the microphones in the flying toilet. And the toilet was now suddenly let go, falling headlong, with the big star inside. At a certain moment, the bungee cords grew taut and, before touching the ground, the toilet shot back upwards, pulled by the elastic force. A fountain of brown and yellow spewed out… The crowd screamed in exultation.

Lona realized that now was not the time to play Vivaldi. She helplessly dropped her bow and violin.

The Mad Reciter passed by her. He was still going on with his Kafka, with "A Hunger Artist": "because I couldn't find the food I liked. If I had found it, believe me, I should have made no fuss and stuffed myself like you or anyone else!"

Lona started to cry.

The fireflies of Central Park came out alongside her, gently whispering of childhood.

A few squirrels appeared, came closer, but once they figured out there was no food, only a violin, they went back to their elm trees all around.

Lona followed them with her eyes out of habit, her teary gaze slid towards the crowns of the trees and glimpsed the sky. Now it was low, starless, covered with thick dark clouds that mixed with the smoke from the fireworks and smothered all light coming from below.

"A greedy sky," she thought.

One red rocket split off from the fireworks, turned over Central Park, flashed above Lona, then headed towards the bay in front of Manhattan and quietly died out, right above the Statue of Liberty.

Bulgarian Weasel Hound

Old Banerjee came by the lake again. Another beautiful spring morning in Southern Illinois. Red robins whistling through the neighbor's garden. An woodpecker in the old walnut tree. Tom-tit by the oak. A ring ouzel in the elm tree.

Old Banerjee looked up with some joy to the promising lacework of the clear blue sky above the lake and above the world.

Then he whistled for the dog. Pomeran came to him, sniffing the ground and the bushes.

- Ok, boy, lets have our little walk again.

They started together by the lake's shore. They passed the small deck occupied by rods and reels. They gazed for a while at the old boat slightly rocking by the deck. And they moved on to explore their free land. Something they have been doing for the past fourteen years, ever since Old Banerjee retired from his job as a lung surgeon.

Long time ago he came to America from India. He was wise and skilled. He managed to get a well-paid job. He married a beautiful American girl. Some fifty years ago. They raised four kids, four great sons. Now all of them had started their own life, living with their spouses and kids, Old Banerjee's grand-children. All sons were doing well. All of the boys. And now Old Banerjee realized he has just turned seventy-seven this morning. Probably his wife, Janet, was preparing for a surprising party in the evening. But now it was just the very beginning of a beautiful Spring day. Another day in his fruitful and wise life. Seventy-seven. And Pomeran was actually fourteen already. Not bad for a dog.

- Hey, Banerjee, good morning! – the rich neighbor, Kimberly, stood by the lake, walking her two high-breed English hounds. Each of them cost fifteen thousand dollars. Kimberly was a banker. She participated in several banking boards in California. She had a cozy house in San Francisco, a yacht, and plenty of shares in different New York financial institutions. She would spend every other month in Southern Illinois to rest a bit from the nervous wounds of the financial jungle.

"They actually cost more than a car," thought Banerjee.

- And a good morning to you, Kimberly, he replied.

Kimberly made her typical funny face and looked at her dogs. Then she gazed at the lake. Then she kept silent, thinking of something.

"There we go again," thought Old Banerjee. "She is thinking of some new way to irritate me for my dog being a cross-breed. She has been doing this for the past ten years. And I keep on finding some indefinite answers. But today is my birthday. And I should think of some worthy and matching response to her foxy attacks."

- Listen, Banerjee, Kimberly said. I have always asked you about the origin of your dog, Pony…

- His name is not Pony, his name is Pomeran, replied Old Banerjee.

- Yes, yes, indeed, Pomeran, I am sorry. I know he is a great dog. But I also now he is not from a particular breed, is that right?

"Ah… Some things never change," thought Banerjee.

- I have always hated the word "mud," Kimberly said and made a lukewarm smile. It is not fair to use it for a man or for an animal. But could we say that your dog is a "lurcher"? It is a British word for cross-breed hunting dogs, she explained.

Old Banerjee, though, has decided he could have a battle today. "No remorse this time," he said to himself. "And no pity."

- Actually, this is a dog of a single and a very noble breed, he said.

He could see how Kimberly's face was glowing reddish and then it faded to a scary pale.

- Really? And what is its breed then? Kimberly bit the left corner of her upper lip.

- Well, he is a Bulgarian Weasel Hound. They are very rare and very hard to find and buy in Europe. They cost twenty thousand euro, and according to the present exchange rate, this is about thirty thousand in US dollars. Not counting the shipping fees.

- Oh, Banerjee, my headache is killing me again. I gotta go back, take my pills and lye down for a while. Have a nice day! And, turning sharply around, Kimberly headed fast about her house, followed by the English hounds.

Old Banerjee looked at the lye water by the shore of the lake and smiled.

On the next day Kimberly took the first flight to San Francisco. It has been almost a year since Old Banerjee's seventy-seventh birthday party, and yet nobody has seen her in Southern Illinois. Finally, a letter came from Kimberly to some of her neighbors by the lake. She said California was better healing her tremendous headache.

Mozart in Prague

Dedicated to the great Wolfgang Amadeus Mozart (1756 - 1791). I bow to his memory, may it live on in eternal light!

Prague loved Mozart. No matter how downtrodden and insulted he might be in Vienna, the more cruelly his evil-wishers from the emperor's court thrust daggers into his heart, the more the Czechs sincerely delighted in him, ecstatically welcoming his music. For them, Mozart was a cherished friend. And the pack of malicious courtiers was joined by imperial composers and mediocre appointed lackeys, who swept up all the prizes, were on the front pages of all the Viennese newspapers, and simultaneously played the obscurantist role of jury and claque and censor and prize-winner… Members of a secret society, supposedly Mozart's "brothers," they betrayed him in various ways – from informing on him through an ordinary refusal of friendship and support to high-level intrigues and destruction of the genius' personality.

Mozart believed that art was an altar he served. Offended and despairing from the poison they pumped into his veins, he was always looking for an escape, a change in his fate, enlightenment, love, warmth.

He managed to arrange for the premiere of "Don Giovanni" in Prague. Citizens of the hundred-spired golden Bohemian capital were overjoyed and immediately bought up all the tickets. On the day of the premiere, the opera was filled with exalted devotees of Mozart.

And the day arrived. The overture rang out. The auditorium resounded with applause and cries: "Bravo, maestro!" The first act began. Prague was happy. Europe was happy. Mozart was on his way to victory in his lifetime.

But in the middle of the first act, the empress stood up and shouted: "Porcheria!"[1]

Mozart's heart sank. The performance was called off. The premiere was ruined by an imperial personage who had come especially from Vienna, from the capital of her beloved empire. It was a monstrous blow. Prague felt pain. The Czechs cried along with their suffering friend. The authorities had violated their most cherished relationship, which, however, turned out to be eternal. Two hundred years later, a Czech with a highly enlightened and elevated soul, Miloš Forman, would go to America and create there the most magnificent work of art ever dedicated to the genius' fate — the film *Amadeus*.

That same evening, Mozart and Constanze set out for Vienna. They passed over the Charles Bridge. The carriage reached the figure of the Crucifixion.

"Stop!" Mozart cried.

The coachman abruptly yanked on the reins.

He got out of the carriage and knelt on the bridge, right next to the eternal cross itself. Above him there were large stars, the universe was quiet, deep, strange.

"Oh my savior!" Mozart turned to Him, choking on groans, weeping, sobbing, shaking. "I have already lost my strength. You know this. You see everything. My heart is bleeding. My soul is sick. I am wasting away. I am becoming invisible. I slam the door on that dusty station where you have sent me among primitive, yet frightening and dangerous creatures. All I have left is the path to You. It pours sweet nectar into a tormented soul and forgives, forgives, forgives… It is the path to the only silence, peace, perfection. I am leaving this place and You know it. Take me into Your starry kingdom, wrap me up, comfort me, far from here. I love everything, everyone, every last blade of grass. I forgive them. I forgive them. I hope You exist, I hope You exist, I

---

1 Filth! (ital.) author's note.

hope You exist. I am now in your Garden of Gethsemane and my tears are dropping on the paving stones, as large as drops of blood. My tears and yours are mixing. I can hear the Requiem. We are crying together. I deliver myself to You now, you grant, and oh do grant me redemption, peace, sweet deliverance. Please give me the strength to leave forgiven. And to arrive forgiven. I see the Light. I see the Meaning. I have praised You my whole life. The pack has crushed my heart because I carried Your spirit. *Now they are crucifying me on the cross.* I love You, my savior. How glorious is our tragedy, glorious, inescapable, fatal. Give life to us all one day, give us life. Forgive me, but I am already coming to You. Accept me with love. Your sky is magnificent!"

And in a whisper he added, cured through suffering, resigned after the horror, calmed in a burst of all-forgiving feeling that always comes after intolerable pain: "And I, too, beneath it! And I, too, beneath it! And I, too, beneath it!"

The coachman and Constanze were white as sheets.

Three months later Mozart returned to the Creator, only stopping by Vienna for a short while on the way.

Jonathan is Playing Chess

My dear ones, brother and sister Europeans! Close and distant relatives, related and unrelated souls! You, from whom I myself and the majority of the communities around me, as well as more than half of the inhabitants of this enormous, vast, great, and prospering country, have originated! You, my grandmothers and grandfathers, aunts and uncles, great-grandmothers and great-grandfathers, cousins! Gorgeous sisters-in-law and daughters-in-law! Kinsfolk from Ireland, Sweden, Germany, England, Italy, Poland, the Czech Republic, Slovakia, but no, not only you, no! I address absolutely all of you in Europe, without exception, since the story I am trying to tell you is in some way important to all of you there and to all of us here.

On both sides of the ocean we are related; and not only through hereditary blood and kinship... It has already been a few centuries (before and after our Independence) in which our common philosophy has been developing, changing and built upon. Well, it vanishes every now and then, but later we always manage to find a way out, don't we? And everything begins and ends up with you. But it can't be otherwise. You have created Hegel, but also Nietzsche! Dostoyevsky, but also Machiavelli! Beethoven, but also Wagner! You have composed the communist Manifesto, but you have also expertly portrayed Your Kampf, haven't you? You have provided us with the experience of "Simon, Fourie & Owen Limited", but also with that of Rothschild—Unlimited! You have managed to create in good time the manufacture, the cartel, the usury, the colonies, but we have giftedly adopted and recreated the cartels into corporations, the rent into bonds, and the colonies into a nation of United States. With direct democracy. And, my dear ones, since now, here at the studio, someone is giving me a hint that a rhyme has just popped up, I am going to ask our two rappers, who are our guests at our radio in NYC: a white-like-me brother rapper from Bulgaria, the continent of Europe, and an Afro-American, or to say it otherwise, a black-like-me brother rapper from Los Angeles, CA. We are going to ask them to quickly knock together a verse. You may ask why I say white and black like me? Well, because my origin is unique: I am simultaneously a proud English-Irishman from Albion, a proud Jew from Slovakia, a proud, snow-white Swedish-Boer from Scandinavia, and a very, very proud black Titan from Ghana and SAR, from Mother Africa and from Harlem in New York City. Here they go; listen to them:

Yeah, yeah, yes,

From Europe to the US,
all the money of the bless'd
got its best interest:
the cartel is corporation
rent's become obligation,
colony is a democracy,
there's more, just look'n see!
And since this radio is heard
through the Web around the world,
we'll sing to this rhyme
sublime:

to the US—
    yeah, yeah, yes,
        God bless, God bless,
and to Europe—
    yah, yah, ya-a-h,
        and ha-ha-ha-a-a...
        Ha-ha-ha!

Thank you, brothers! Now go away from the mike—fast! For this is a serious broadcast.

You have raised our spirits a little. Perhaps we needed it, perhaps we didn't. But anyway, don't expect a new invitation from me until next month. As far as what the brother rappers sing is concerned, dear listeners, Europeans and Americans, it is true. From here, from New York City, from the heart of the Manhattan-Harlem connection, we are broadcasting to all of Europe as well. We hold six percent of the audience in Manhattan, four in Quincy, three in Bro-o-o-klyn and whole two percent in the Bronx! Don't look condescendingly with your one-and-a-half percent, European brothers! Since we are keen on having an intelligent audience, and since broadcasts like mine are becoming increasingly rare both here and there, don't gloat over it! We are not out for percentages. We will broadcast as long as we can. But we won't change ourselves! And personally I am not going to surrender! Look here, I have prepared a terrific story for you again tonight. It is important to both sides of the Atlantic. However, first let me make it clear for the last time: you over there, Europeans, don't be condescending towards American intellect! Brooklyn alone will contain London! Manhattan alone will swallow up Paris! If that doesn't satisfy you, we'll throw Rome into Quincy, Berlin into the Bronx, and we'll spread Vienna onto Staten Island, and there will still be space left next to it for a Madrid or two together with Lisbon! We are your offspring, so, respect us! You'll see for yourselves that if we don't answer some questions together now, we'll keep failing later and forever. Again together. That is why you need to listen carefully from now on.

* * *

Jonathan came from Ethiopia. He was tall and had exceptionally regular features with the radiance of a revolutionary intellectual from restless Africa. His eyes had a serene look with a sense of a certain future. His forehead was high and domed. His matte skin was thin and delicate. His hair formed a fluffy, curly cloud, slightly gray here and there not due to age, but as a result of tribulations, hardships and early-come wisdom. In fact, you could recognize Jonathan by the hair: it stood on his head like a funnel with the wide end turned towards the Universe, and from there the Creator could pour instructions directly into him.

Yes, dear European listeners, I can hear your aesthetic feelings purring. No, I don't mean to say that you're snobs. Let's not split right now and call each other names like "Negroes" or "snobs", OK? You're right that I used the same word twice. But I have no other way out if I want to describe Jonathan properly to you. Yes, he is tall, and his forehead is high too. I can't say simply "domed". Or that Jonathan is "well-built". No. He is tall. With a high brow. With high hair. When you look at him he stands up somehow high in front of you. When he begins to speak to you, you sense a high spirit. When he laughs, you communicate with an elevated soul. When you get to know him, you feel and experience high ideas. If you see him angry and struggling with life, you will be convinced for the umpteenth time that the world will continue to be unjust for a long time. That's why reason is looking for height to stand on and see around, far and wide, in all four directions, with irresistible force. High force.

Jonathan had been living in New York for eleven years. About to be killed in his motherland, he had managed to escape aboard a ship sailing from the port of Eritrea. He graduated with a degree in philosophy from Columbia University, with the help of some kind of foundation. Since he was always moneyless, he managed to remain for years at one of the housing facilities of Columbia, somewhere between Manhattan and Harlem. Everyone knew him and sheltered him. Moreover, that housing facility was quite different from the rich country campuses. There was space in the country: acres and acres of grass, buildings, libraries, swimming pools, tennis courts, cinemas, restaurants and all the rest. But this was New York City, brothers. There wasn't a single free place here, and everything was vertical. That was why the campus of Columbia University was vertical, too. It had a swimming pool, a fitness center, a movie theater, a football field and a tennis court, and all those were hanging over at various breathtaking, gray-brown levels among the rest of the concrete mountains. Due to the narrowness, everything was kind of "micro" (and in New York there was "macro" only for a few people): the rooms were sixty-five square feet each (like Raskolnikov's, you know), and there was a common bathroom on each level of this thirty-story student skyscraper.

Something typical for New York had befallen that vertical campus. In this favorite city of ours, there are ongoing beginnings from great ideas: Art Deco, Mies Van Der Rohe, etc. But alas, the principles according to which we have constructed our civilization are in reality brutally iron-strong. And rule number one is: "Living, constructing, creating, and showing entrepreneurship, resourcefulness, ingenuity or even just ordinary capacity for work, are only allowed if divided into units of time, provided such a niche has been allocated. Boring a new niche is prohibited. Well, yes, dear Europeans, if you don't trust me, when you happen to come to New York, take a walk along Fifth Avenue (There it is, in front of me…), stop at Rockefeller Plaza (Ah, we got even with you for Rothschild with this Rockefeller!), and have a look at the gold plate. Rockefeller principles are written down on it; in gold letters at that. You know what I mean? Gold upon gold. Pay attention to the following shining principle of precious metal:

> "I believe in the dignity of labor, whether with head or hand;
> that the world owes no man a living but that it owes every man
> an opportunity to make a living."

You see my dear ones? The man formulated it so honestly. He managed in good time to lay his hands on oil, fill his pockets with gold flowing out of the drills, and he got sixty percent of all those free opportunities he stands for. So, the next one got thirty percent of the opportunities, and the third in this business got the last ten percent. And the niche was filled! And so on, niche after niche. They got proportionally filled up.

There is such a method in mathematics: the divisor method. First you use a big divisor, then a smaller and smaller one, until you reach down to one. But even math proves that, using this method, whoever gets the largest part at the beginning continues to get the most, right up to the last fraction...

So that's what happened in the case with the vertical campus where Jonathan lived: at first they wanted to make it a big and spacious skyscraper like the Chrysler Building (even back then they knew that it would not be as big as the Empire State Building), but there had been only a small niche left for the needs of the University of Columbia and its students. So it was nice that they could at least have that in the end. They laughed themselves at the end. At the opening a professor said: "Well, we started from Art Deco and Van Rue, and we ended with Pirsig's little cubicles..."

So, my dear ones, Europeans and Americans of all kinds, back to Jonathan. In addition to living in this miracle of architecture and social philosophy, which I guess I described to you by all possible means, Jonathan earned his living with... chess. He played in several clubs professionally, but that income was absolutely insufficient to him, and mainly unstable, since the money came only when tournaments were organized. The club owners did not pay wages to their chess players, nor did they provide training for them. First, they had to be really very good to find a club, and second, they had to be lucky enough to be entered in at least one medium-category tournament. Most of those were petty, local events with little advertising (accordingly, with low profit). Moreover, every participant owed forty percent to the sponsors and forty percent to the club owner.

Do you remember what I was explaining to you about the niches, my dear ones? Well, now you yourselves are an example, because, as you in Europe say (except for the English, because they cook tastelessly and with too little salt.

They have a specially-formed negative attitude to salt, based on which they created an entire drama:"King Lear), "a rule without an example is like soup without salt". The individual players in this chess niche were allocated twenty percent of all the free opportunities proclaimed, manifested, no, dear listeners, rather offered, by Rockefeller.

So. Even if you have already turned off the radios and the computers, I continue over the ether of consciousness.

Jonathan was forced to play additionally, illegally, of course. He knew all the secret gambling refuges in Manhattan and Harlem, quite a number in Quincy and Staten Island, and some in Brooklyn, while those in Bronx he avoided like plague.

Generally speaking, my dear brother and sister Europeans, now is the moment to tell you one more brutal truth. When you hear "New York City", I swear to you, both in the name of the Creator and of the Anti-molder, do not call to mind your favorite Max Frisch! Our real, enormous, strange, unsleeping, fire-spitting giant and master—this City of the Lack of a Cult —it is not the illuminated signs of cheese crackers of your Mister Frisch, it is not the shallow chants of Senghor. Don't be tempted by Sinatra or Lisa Minnelli either! Don't succumb to shilly-shallying like "The Big Apple" and the ravings from Soho of similar artists. Don't listen to your loose, spineless and shaky diplomats, journalists, singers and poets, who come here for a while and later hum and babble immature nonsense to you about "the category", "the memory", "the annihilation" and the like; a lot of nonsense!

I will only tell you one thing about it. I, the one born in its Heart. This city leaves you speechless.

And just try to think at least for a while without words. Come on, try it! Break up every single thought in your head! Let me hear you! Test your reason! Embrace thought! When you find a solution to this dilemma, call me at the studio. Here, between Manhattan and Harlem, I am still searching, waiting and hoping to get an Answer some time.

* * *

Everyone on the Columbia campus loved Jonathan. He captivated them because he did not play the coquet with his ideas. He told them about the sufferings of his people. He shared with them stories about the sorrowful plight of many other peoples from one end of the variegated cradle of Africa to the other. He openly declared himself against Wall Street, the Exchange, the big corporations, the financial sharks, the never ending new wars. But he never talked about ecology and anti-globalism. He would argue with his friends, who took part in such rallies and demonstrations throughout the world. He would explain to them that they would not achieve anything that way, and that in addition, they were used to compromising unwillingly and in front of all world cameras, the value of true ideas. He would tell them that "globalism" was a convenient substitute for the true term: "capitalism, growing into imperialism". He insisted that when things were not called by their true names, later the meaning of the struggle itself would be replaced, and this would inevitably result in failure. "Since at the Beginning was the Word, according to John", Jonathan liked to say. "And John was right. While any euphemism dooms us to a fake trumpet and turns us into cowards."

They really loved him so much that even when he slapped Mr. Jing, the owner of the Korean restaurant, in the face because he didn't pay him the twenty dollars due to him for honestly winning two out of three games, even then they found a way to save him from the frightful district cop, the fat Bonny-Scott Carter, to whom Mr. Jing had made a complaint. They hid Jonathan in the movie theater warehouse. Although Bonny-Scott walked all thirty stories with a forty-five caliber "Colt" stuck to his ass, and the handcuffs with which he intended to arrest Jonathan, he nevertheless missed the improvised hiding place. Finally, at the exit onto the busy street, panting and red-faced, he said to them under his nose, tucking his right thumb into his belt and waving a warning with his left forefinger at their grinning faces:

"I know you well! Students' solidarity, uh? Revolutionaries, uh? Anti-globalists… I know he's somewhere around here. But anyway…" Bonny-Scott spat on the sidewalk of Amsterdam Avenue, then turned around and flopped into the huge police Chevy. The car sagged a little and tilted over to the driver's side. Everyone knew that Bonny-Scott, poor fellow, was a very poor, but extremely keen lover of chess. Pulling away from the curb, he rolled down the side-window of the Chevy and announced to them with dignity:

"But I'll get hold of you some time down there at Times Square during some of your demonstrations! And pray it is I, for at least we know each other…"

He turned on the red and blue lights to bully the traffic and to join sharply its mad flow, and dashed off somewhere in the direction of Columbus Circle to drink a Doctor Pepper to ease his soul.

On a warm, sunny, sagacious and smiling October day of year 2000, Jonathan was sitting and playing chess "for fixed" (with a small bet, between two and five dollars) at an outdoor café by the lake in Central Park. He was taking away the pennies of keen middle class amateurs, who had come to spend the Saturday in the open.

Ducks were floating on the lake. Children were throwing them crumbs of bread and candies. The whole park was glowing in red. The tree leaves rolled a little to show everyone their brightness, outlined distinctly in the transparent air.

On the lawn above the lake, on the still green grass, stood Schiller's bust, erected by the German Society in America. In a semicircle behind it, charming tree crowns, fascinated, continued to tremble in red, orange, yellow and purple, reminding the passersby:

Beauty will save the world!

Suddenly, a fifty-some year-old man in a gray suit, with expensive platinum glasses through which were looking a pair of unflinching eyes, also steel-gray like the armored door of a mighty Wall Street safety vault, approached Jonathan's table with dignity.

"Mr. Jonathan?" the stranger asked.

"Yep. Blood and flesh. What can I do for you?"

"My pleasure. My name is Glacerbell. Mr. Coldman, Jr. has sent me."

"Coldman... Like that Coldman?"

"Yes, Simon Coldman, who has sent me, is the son of Mr. Henry Coldman himself. That is why he is Junior."

"Aha, I see. But I don't grasp how much good am I to the biggest banking shark on Wall Street."

"Not to him, only to the Junior. Mr. Coldman himself doesn't know anything about this conversation."

"Okay, but how much good am I to the Junior Billionaire?"

"Jonathan, would you agree to meet him? He will acquaint you with his proposal. He insists on doing it in person."

"H'm, I don't remember owing him any debts..."

"No, you don't. Take someone to accompany you. Someone you trust to serve as a witness and a sport second."

"Ah, I think I am guessing. All right, when and where?"

"If it's to your convenience, tomorrow morning at ten sharp Mr. Coldman will be expecting you in his office in Wall Street. You know the building... It's world-known... The security will be alerted. Mr. Coldman Jr.'s office premises are on the seventeenth floor. Those of Mr. Henry Coldman are on the twenty-fifth. I am telling you this as a curious detail, since only a few from the entire global world have entered there. And only a couple of those few are New Yorkers."

"But tomorrow is Sunday!"

"Exactly. Mr. Henry Coldman himself will not be in the building all day long, since he will be resting for sure. You will have the chance to talk at ease with Mr. Simon. I will attend too. And you bring along your man. Please, be on time, both of you."

"Understood. Good bye, Mr. Glacerman."

"Glacerbell."

"My apologies, Glacerbell…"

"See you tomorrow, Jonathan."

Dear Europeans, when the name Coldman is only uttered, whole ranks of people stand to attention from Baltimore to Kuala Lumpur! An incredible shark! A true magnate! This is why you need to stay tuned!

* * *

The Sunday morning on Wall Street was quiet, peaceful, free of any stress, un-businesslike and extremely human. There were no hurrying financiers, Lincolns or brokers. Here and there the light breeze was tossing around the Friday edition of the "Times". There were tourists walking about, and two Italians were selling them bagels. All the banks and the exchange were closed. In front of, and behind, their invincible doors paced self-assured security guards equipped with automatic weapons.

Jonathan had taken with him Mer-Lin, a talented young philosopher, ethnic Chinese born in Malaysia. He had lived there, and in Brunei, and finally in New York, graduating from Columbia University.

Coldman and Glacerbell were waiting for them. Behind the gigantic window panes opened the magnificent view of Manhattan, the area in the visible Universe sheltering the largest percentage of top brass. One could see clearly the Twin Towers of the World Trade Center, the New York

Exchange, the office buildings of Lehman Brothers, J. P. Morgan, Salomon Brothers, Chase Manhattan, Battery Park, Fisher-Stanley, First National, City Group…

They were served coffee. Jonathan was even allowed to light a cigarette. Glacerbell and Mer-Lin did not smoke, but Coldman produced a cigarillo with the fragrance of Indian fern.

"It's lucky that today the old man is away and I can smoke at ease!"

Simon Coldman leaned back in his leather armchair. It looked as if he were leaning proprietarily through thin air on the whole heap of steel and glass behind his back. And the more comfortably his throne enveloped him, the more his torso faded behind the huge palisander desk. Only his head was visible, hanging down in the spacious vast azure above Manhattan.

"Jonathan, I propose to you a chess duel. Here are our seconds", he described a semicircle towards Glacerbell and Mer-Lin.

"So I supposed yesterday. I have happened to hear about your hobbies, sir…"

"Call me Simon, Jonathan. Let's escape from the paranoia of officialdom. Call me Simon."

"H'm, excuse me, sir, but let's rather not act childishly. There is a crucial precipice, an abyss between us, and hypocritical familiarity, you know it even better than I do, won't fill it…"

"Oh, well, let's say I know it. So be it. But, you will at least admit, sir, that in our native English language it is exactly the feigned tone of a slight official pompousness, combined by all means with a veneration evoking paranoia, which creates that invisible implicit difference between the polite and the ordinary form of address. Something, which in the other languages is allowed lexically, is left in ours to the tone, to the meaning, to the context, to the pretext, if you like. Excuse me, but in the field of linguistics I am even more leftist than you! Ha-ha!"

"I don't have the slightest doubt about it."

"I do not tell lies, Jonathan. Unlike many other children of billionaires (I know dozens of them), I am neither hypocrite, nor madman, nor drug addict, nor dullard, nor weakling, nor failed, weak-minded, spoiled fool. I stand firmly for the principles of the class from which I come. I do not oppose wealth and money. I am a firm adherent of everything *you hate*: capitalism, globalism, imperialism. Yes, I am convinced that wars are inevitable. No, I do not think that everyone on this Earth is useful, except as a unit of a market of consumers. But in the name of an agitation of the market, part of those millions of ants can be sacrificed. To me, they are despicable straw, a padding of creation, coupling little creatures. Human scrap."

"Coldman, spare me these effusions, if you please. Your imperialistic treatise, lacking hypocrisy, as you yourself say, won't soothe the weak. The only use of it is that it induces more quickly fury in the strong ones among the weak, who have already become sufficiently aware that their only escape is to eliminate not just you or individuals like you, but specifically your class, of which you are so proud!"

"Perfectly right! And true!" Coldman started furiously sipping his coffee and sucking at his cigarillo. "And one such, clearly manifested leader—strong among the weak— according to me, are you! I have been watching you for a long time."

Coldman stood up and walked with a kingly manner to the middle of his celestial office. A huge marble elephant with gold ears, gold nails and gold end of his trunk was sitting there. Coldman crossed his arms on his chest and leaned back in a lordly manner on the mighty front left leg of the elephant.

"And now, dear Jonathan, from now on I am going to call you Jonathan, and as far as what you'll call me is concerned, it's up to you! I propose to you the following. Is everyone listening carefully?"

Glacerbell and Mer-Lin nodded affirmatively.

Jonathan kept silent imperturbably. His eyes not only did not express fury, but were smiling. His entire looks at the moment irradiated rather playfulness.

"Jonathan, if you beat me at chess I will write you a check for ten thousand dollars. But!" Coldman raised his brows and his right forefinger. "But do you care to hear the counter condition? Specifically what it was that made me choose you for a duel?"

"Naturally. Shoot, Coldman! I am all ears, since I don't have an amount to respond to your stake anyway."

"Oh, three hundred angels on the point of a needle! Of course you don't have it! But even if you did have it, you know that it would not be your ten grand that would feed the Wall Street beast, ha-ha-ha! If you lose… Ha-ha… If you lose by any chance… I will ask you to publicly renounce your Marxism, to declare all revolution an anathema, to acknowledge globalism and to proclaim before your friends that the only possible, complete, and final stage of any society is capitalism combined with liberal democracy!"

A diamond clock on an ebony pyramid chimed resonantly and with crystal vibrancy twelve strokes.

"Do you agree?"

"I agree."

"Good! Let's specify the regulations! I suggest the rule "victory in three of five games". I suggest the total time limit for each game to be thirty minutes—fifteen minutes each for all moves. Thus theoretically (although I don't believe we'll reach that far, ha-ha-ha!) the total time is five by three, namely equal to a hundred and fifty minutes or two hours and a half, right?"

"Perfect."

"OK then. A few more details. Halfway—a half hour break?"

"Agreed."

"Seconds, did you get it?"

"Yes, sir!" jumped up Glacerbell.

"We got it." Mer-Lin confirmed.

"Any questions?"

"Just one." Jonathan stood up to leave with Mer-Lin.

"Coldman is listening" Coldman said grinning. "Higher stake?"

"No. But what happens in case the game ends in a draw?"

"Ha, I expected this question. First, I'll beat you, and you know it. Ha-ha-ha! And second…"

"Is there going to be a tiebreaker?" Jonathan cut him sharp.

"No, there won't be. Because, if you by any chance manage to work your way to a draw, that will be no satisfaction to me. The fact that you won't receive my ten thousand won't at all make me happy either. Only tonight I'll spend that much with a charming Rebecca, exquisite and enthralling… My problem will be that you won't have lost. Then my counter condition fails too. And it is very, very important to me."

"I see. Goodbye, Coldman."

"Goodbye. Day of the week, hour, place, arbiter, etc.—Glacerbell will take care of the details and will inform you in good time. And remember, everyone, it's cloak-and-dagger, ha-ha!"

The armed guards escorted them politely along the corridors, in the elevator, all the way to the ground floor, and through the exit onto the quiet Wall Street, Jonathan and Mer-Lin returned to their destined existence.

* * *

This chess duel in New York City will be remembered for a long time, my dear ones!

It took place in an old, but mighty, English colonial building midway between Manhattan and Harlem, not too far from Riverside Drive and the Hudson River, not too far from Amsterdam Avenue and not too far from the Columbia campus. It was a huge, former king's library with thick, stone columns and Gothic, high vaults. It was a proud building with over fifteen stories equal to at least twenty-five present day floors. At one end a breathtaking square tower of cut granite shot up, ending at the top in a spacious widening with gray cornices and windows, a tower worthy of any high magician, or at least of some staunch alchemist leading his secret society in search of the absolute.

It was in this particular tower that the battle took place. All sorts of people had secretly heard of it and had come to watch. One to bet illegally, another out of curiosity, a third out of irresistible sports fever, and a fourth to see fallen and humiliated the opponent who was not dear to his heart. Here were all of Jonathan's adherents from the Columbia campus, as well as all the Wall Street offspring: Coldman's associates. However incredulous it may sound, (but it is a fact confirmed by the New History of New York), in the front line in order to see better, stood as large as life with his authoritative paunch: Bonny-Scott Carter himself, and on his ass still hung the large, ubiquitous Colt. In fact, thanks to Bonny-Scotts' devoted enthusiasm, everyone (even Coldman) felt more at ease: first, they were in the building illegally (usually it was kept locked by city hall and had not been used for years), and second, the bets that were being placed at the moment, as well as the entire wager for which they had gathered, would not be appreciated at all by the NYPD because of their dubious legality.

The players took their seats and exchanged glances. It was Sunday again, exactly a week after their meeting at Wall Street. Behind one sat Glacerbel, behind the other—Mer-Lin.

Coldman had brought a small, elegant chess table made of silver, ivory, ebony and mother-of-pearl with unanimated, platinum pieces for the white, and dark gold representing the black.

By their side, evoking serious respect, stood the live figure of the professional chess arbiter Petersen, ensured and paid by Glacerbell especially for the event.

And so, the time had come. Petersen took out of his black briefcase a chess clock: both modern, electric, and traditional, with the red flags that descended to signify the running out of playing time. He set the clock on the table next to the figures arranged in advance and adjusted it for the first game at fifteen minutes for each player. The lot fell to Jonathan to play first with the white.

"Lucky man!" Coldman cried out. "This means a certain advantage for you, since, hypothetically, if we reach to five games, you'll have played with the white three whole games, and I only two! However, it can't be helped; you have revolutionary luck, ha-ha-ha!"

"Gentlemen," Petersen said, "I won't stop you from talking during the game, but, in the first place, I'll ask you to talk quietly, and secondly, I'll watch the conversation for offensive language, provocations and unsportsmanlike tricks."

"OK, Petersen! Shall we begin?"

It turned out that Coldman was a strong, experienced, imperious, hurricane sort of an opponent. In his youth he had been in chess professionally with the idea of fighting to enter the League, but later, due to his father's ambitions to take over the business, he had had to give it up and "fall into line" with Wall Street society. From the very first game, Jonathan felt that this opponent surpassed him in some quality. It was as if he was trying to tame a wild bronco, one that was stomping powerfully with his hoofs, did not fit the stereotypes of classical logic, and was impossible to dupe or to make a party to the hidden philosophy of a certain combination; what is more, he would not let himself fall into a trap, nor was it possible to outplay him by a brutal attack in the Mittelspiel.

Nevertheless, due to his inner conviction that he could not be overpowered by Coldman, Jonathan put all his efforts into winning the first game. He did manage to, but it was a victory like one in which you drain your own self of blood as a military commander, battering to pieces the mechanism of your entire army to the point where you become transparent to the enemy. On top of everything, he noticed that Coldman played faster than he and saved time for the Endspiel. When he finally checkmated Coldman, the billionaire had seven whole minutes left, while Jonathan had only thirteen seconds! It was all to the good that he noticed his opponent's thriftiness when it came to time. Otherwise, it could have played a dirty trick on him.

In the second and third games Coldman showed himself to be a Titan; to be a unique symbiosis between Morphy and Bobby Fischer. Thrifty in the openings, he was terrible in the Mittelspiel. As faultless as a cyber machine, he dealt insidious combinations destroying and guessing every possible resistance or counterattack. As sly as a fox, he constantly searched for "forks", "pins" and "X-rays". One had to be endlessly careful with him; it was like playing against a computer. Coldman's approach to the Sicilian Defense was furious, with a concept of his own. He responded to Queen's Gambit with Queen's Gambit, but against the King's Gambit he did not allow "white batteries", he would deliberately destroy the center, and if need be in the name of a quicker victory and of working his way to the opponent's King's camp, he would sacrifice his own castling, becoming twice as dangerous in the attack. It was harder for him to fight against the Old Indian Defense, and in that case he would waste a lot of time thinking over how to attack. Eventually Coldman won the second and third games. And he achieved everything as early as the Mittelspiel. He was just one victory away from smashing Jonathan completely.

The fourth game was the first in which they actually reached an Endspiel. This time Coldman made a tactical mistake, although he had a pawn more, and in theory all was lost for Jonathan. Obviously, Coldman was a great strategist, but he wasn't very good at math. They had only the Kings and some pawns left. Jonathan had four; Coldman—five. However, the billionaire had miscalculated the moves of the Kings, which were at parity. He was forced to allow the enemy's King to the rear of his own pawns. He lost three of them. The remaining two were blocked by Jonathan's. Two pawns of the Ethiopian marched calmly and undisturbed forward to the final line to become Queens. Then Coldman surrendered.

The score became even: two points each.

The decisive fifth game remained.

Jonathan was playing with the white pieces, the platinum ones.

He began with Old Indian Defense. He was feeling rather close to losing and exceptionally unsure of himself. He was scared in good earnest. Even though playing with the whites, he gave up any attacks and aggression. He chose an exceptionally defensive mode taking into account two things. First, the Old Indian Defense made Coldman angry. He wanted to smash the opponent fast, but that was exactly why he wasted time thinking every detail of his offensive over carefully, since he knew that in this debut offensive was not at all easy, and was hiding a multitude of sunken rocks for the attacker. And second, Jonathan himself saw to win seconds at every single move. At this final sprint he was going to reckon on Time: the chief arbiter of the human race in general, and of chess-players in particular.

The fire-spitting dragon Coldman came down on Jonathan like a hawk on a sparrow: a tearing attack aimed directly at the King's flank. He began to break through the defense and to transfer reinforcements from the reserves and from the other flank where nothing was happening anyway.

While playing, they continued to fire words at one another:

"Looks like the end is approaching, man." Coldman said shaking his head in the rhythm of blues to tease him. "If you only knew how I'm waiting to see the end of your Marxism! Oh!"

The arbiter, Petersen, made attempts to stop such conversations, but the crowd began to shout so frantically, that Petersen, like an old conservative conductor, was forced to cut at least the crescendos off.

"You know, Simon", Jonathan spoke out suddenly as well. "One Christmas night, you know what Christmas is, don't you? I was homeless at the time, walking along Fifth Avenue with nowhere to go. I stopped in front of Rockefeller Plaza. An ordinary little fellow with a Christmas songbook in his hands was gathering occasional passersby around him. I joined them. I began to sing Christmas carols together with them:

On the first day of Christmas,
My true love sent to me…

And so on, you know it."
"So what?"
"So nothing. It was nice. Only, a cop drove us away."
"Why?"
"Well, he referred to some text from the city statutes. More than so-and-so-many people at the same place without advance permission from the city hall, etc…. Sheer nonsense! Meanwhile, the people were simply singing Christmas carols pleasing to God and to America."
"A-ha, now you're going to say that the cop was white, right?"
"Tell you the truth, he was white. And there was a woman cop with him. They were a street patrol couple."
"A-ha. And she too was white, wasn't she?"
"No, she, on the other hand, was black, blacker then me. And she was meaner than her colleague to the folks. In

the end, she herself drove us decisively, even aggressively, away."

"How about the people, what were they? White?"

"White, black, yellow, all sorts. A colorful Christmas time crowd."

"U-huh. And what happened later?"

"Later, since I was on Rockefeller Plaza anyway, I decided for the last time in my life to cast a glance at those detestable Jesuit principles of his, inscribed in gold letters on a gold plate."

"And did you look at them?"

"I walked to the plate. There were two girls standing in front of it."

"Black? White?"

"One was white, the other black."

"And what happened?"

"Ah, how could they have chosen exactly the one Rockefeller's "principles" I hate most of all. I forgot what number it was; you know, the Jesuit has numbered them on top of that, don't you? To make things worse, they also were lost in admiration of it and were even reading it out loud!"

"Well, I too have forgotten their numbers. But why don't you refresh my memory, if you please?"

"Oh, well, listen, everybody:

"I believe in the dignity of labor, whether with head or hand;
that the world owes no man a living but that it owes every man
an opportunity to make a living."

"Well, you see, the guy has put it very well!"

"Ah, we would have really been surprised to hear a different evaluation from the mouth of the humanist Coldman!" Jonathan cried out.

Everyone laughed.

"But wait", Coldman would not become quiet. "Who was reading the inscription to whom? The white one to the black?"

"No, the truth is—the black was reading it to the white. Moreover, it was exactly the black one, who discovered exactly that principle for herself and at that moment exactly she was lost in admiration and read it out loud. And in the end she said: "I really like this one!""

"Well, what does that tell you? Doesn't it finally reveal the lie to you?"

"Of course not. She was just the umpteenth soul of an invisible betrayer: well-stagnated, well-formatted to believe that she was equal, that everything was going to be a fairytale, if only she followed without deviating from the track the formula of happiness that had been drawn when she was a child."

"Did you by any chance tell her something like this?"

"No, I didn't. But you're right: I could not restrain myself and keep my mouth totally shut. For even the purest reason is shaken before that slave girl."

"Wow! How poetic and categorical you appear to be! But what did you tell her, after all?"

"Unexpectedly to myself and the two girls, tempted to cross my sword with the no less powerful sword of stupidity, I spoke out. There, on Rockefeller Plaza, in front of the gold of the plate at the foot of the gigantic skyscraper of your brother-in-class, my thought focused on and situated in that instance of the existence of the Universe. All I wanted to give them was another well-known quote from Rockefeller 'The way to make money is to buy when blood is running in the streets.' But all I said was: 'For Pete's sake, not on this night! At least not on Christmas, for God's sake! Jesus Christ is being born, you understand?' And I walked away along Fifth Avenue."

"H'm, now why are you telling me this about Jesus Christ? Because you know that I am a Jew and you want to annoy me, right?"

"No. And you have to know something else. All right, you are a Jew. As for me, I am Judean. But that does not prevent me from loving Jesus Christ."

"What? You? Judean? Are you now mocking me?"

"I am not mocking you at all. Your brutal prejudice prevents you from believing me at this moment only because I am black."

"Wait, where do you come from?"

"From Ethiopia."

"Ah. It seems there were there those…"

"There were, there are and there yet will be. Abyssinian Judeans. Some have even been admitted to Israel. All the better that it didn't depend on those like you. You would have left them to starve to death."

"Enough of that. It can't be that bad."

"Ha, you think *we* don't know? You see now? There is no Judean conspiracy. There are only ideas and a struggle of ideas. Whichever wins over later is accused of conspiracy. At the moment your ideas are about to be accused, since they've gotten the upper hand here and there in the world, mostly in Eastern Europe. Therefore, your turn is coming now. And your move." Jonathan moved his chessman then pressed sharply the button of his half of the ticking chess-clock.

"Damn it! I'll exterminate you!" Coldman was getting furious.

Otherwise, the extermination was coming close. Jonathan remained with the King and a Rook; Coldman, with a Queen and a pawn. Look, Coldman did a "pin" and took Jonathan's Rook as well! And listen now, dear Europeans and Americans, what happened during that decisive, Gordian game! If you are very interested in it, you can even replay it later at home. I will let you know the moves.

Jonathan had lost everything, but his tactics of saving time paid off. Determined to defeat him quickly, embarking on furious attacks, and at times absentminded as a result of their ideological disputes, in the second half (conditional half, of course, my dear ones; this is no football; don't be confused), Coldman looked more and more rarely at the clock… He pressed the button automatically, carried away by his assault and infuriated by the conversation.

Thus the following situation occurred:

Goldmen had all in all seven seconds left. Jonathan had over a minute, but he had already only one King. Coldman had the King, a Queen and a pawn. He was short of seconds to mate Jonathan with the King and the Queen. He set forward with the pawn. Tick-tick, move. Tick-tick, move. Jonathan simply moved his King peering at the clock. One of them was playing in total Zeitnot, and the other in an odd Zugzwang. The whole tower overcrowded with people watched the clock dial and the little red flag. Petersen, most of all. It appeared that even though completely defeated, Jonathan would win by time.

Tick-tick, move. Stop, Tick-tick, move. Stop of the timer. Tick-tick, move. "Halt, stopwatch! Stop, Time!" Coldman prayed. Tick-tick, stop. Tick-tick, stop.

"Stooooop!" the arbiter cried out.

The little red flag in Coldman's clock dropped down as if cut off. The alarm shrieked, and the dial showed: 0 minutes and 0 seconds.

Everyone crowded around the chessboard, pushing each other unrestrainedly and rudely. Dear listeners, the picture was as follows: Jonathan's white King was on E2. Coldman's black King was on B3. The black's old Queen had gotten frozen on D8—she had been guarding the corridor for the descent of the black pawn. The second black Queen newly hatched from that pawn was standing gracefully on CI, just come out. With the two Queens, Coldman would have needed no more than three or four seconds to checkmate the white King. But he was short of exactly those seconds. Jonathan's timer was showing a whole minute left. He was winning on time.

Now everyone was expecting the arbiter to announce exactly such a victory. Some already hurried to hug and greet Jonathan, but he angrily pushed them away. Coldman sat gloomy and blushing, peering madly into the stopwatch. Others hurried to cash their bets. Some quarreled fiercely.

However, the arbiter Petersen opened his black briefcase imperturbably and calmly, and produced a thick manual of F.I.D.E. He put on his glasses, opened the law-book and pored on it breathing heavily.

The crowd could not bear the tension. All sorts of cries could be heard.

"Time will be time!"

"But material will be material too!"

"Give me back my money, you scoundrel!"

"Coldman, you lost!"

"Jonathan, you are defeated!"

"Coldman! Coldman! Coldman!"

"Jonathan! Jonathan! Jonathan!"

"Gold-man! Gold-man!" applauded rhythmically one of the wings.

"Jo-na-than! Jo-na-than!" the other half of the crowed responded.

"Draw!" Petersen cried out, slammed the book and took off his glasses.

Complete silence set in for a few seconds. Later on their cries could be heard as far as Philadelphia. Some wanted in earnest to beat up the arbiter, while Glacerbell was trying to pacify them.

"How? Why? According to what rules?"

"According to the latest approved. It is written there: 'When there is not enough mating material, a draw shall be adjudged." And since Jonathan has one bear King and has no mating material, it's a draw. That's it."

"And when is it a victory?"

"If he had at least one pawn, then. Hypothetically it can be turned into a Queen and checkmate. If he had kept the rook, it would also have been a victory."

"And what if it were a knight?"

"It's a draw."

"And if it were a bishop?"

"Again a draw. Again there's no mating material."

"Two bishops?"

"Victory. Mate with two bishops has been proven long time ago."

"Two knights?"

"At the moment it reads "a draw", although they are planning to amend it, since mate with two knights is possible although sometimes it takes more than fifty moves."

"To hell with the rules!"

"Coldman, count the money to Jonathan!"

"Jonathan, say you repent for your Marxism!"

"Basta!" Bonny-Scott stood up and cried out. "Rules will be rules! Period!"

Petersen reached in his briefcase again and produced a small laptop. He turned on a chess matrix and entered absolutely the same arguable situation with preciseness to the second. They waited for the judgment of the software approved by F.I.D.E.

"A draw" the word came up on the display and cut off sharply the passions.

The crowd became reconciled.

The watchers dispersed, but even now, years later, no one has forgotten that game. What is more, the story spread around from mouth to mouth and if it continues to spread like this, it will become a true New York legend.

So, my dear listeners, on the threshold of the Twenty-First Century, midway between Manhattan and Harlem,

Coldman and Jonathan ended with a draw disputed by everyone…

However, that chess match tempered both sides for the forthcoming decisive Battle anticipated in the air and in the hearts of everyone.

Let's Be White Brothers

"And believe me, one who has come to know the truth is miserable and adamant." Those were the words with which Ben Gotz, the owner of the coal mines in Indiana, welcomed me, when he finally received me in a huge office that was a mixture of administrative functionality, retro-vulgarity and American kitsch. He had just seen off some visitor of modest, rather unsightly and pitiful appearance. "Yes, truth has its price!" Ben Gotz poured himself, and even me, a glass of russet, twelve-year-old Wild Turkey.

"But, Mr. Gotz, hasn't Balzac said that an enlightened soul prays..."

"Yes, that's right. But, what happens if one devotes oneself only to praying? What happens then?"

"I am not sure, sir."

"You are not sure, because you're young. But I am sixty-three years old and I know: once you devote yourself to praying, you remain roofless, ha-ha-ha!"

"But..."

"No, there is no "but", young man. There is strict logic. There is matter. Life is short, and God has commanded us to enjoy the material things while we are here. Isn't that right? Otherwise, there is no meaning; at least that's how I see things!"

I had travelled nearly two hundred miles in order to meet Gotz. We got acquainted in the sports hall of Southern Illinois University in Edwardsville. To be more precise, it was at the snack bar during the break at a basketball game. Our team, "Saluki Dogs", was playing the "Wolves" from Indiana, and Ben Gotz was their sponsor. In the course of the conversation, he said that I was intelligent, and he invited me to visit him to talk about some very fat prospective job. My earnings as a student were lean; expenditures always found a way to magically beat them. Moreover, Ben Gotz won me with the fact that in his youth he had been a sports commentator. He successfully imitated himself from those years. He created whole radio sketches for me, combining both his aging consciousness and my memories of legendary baseball and football games. In addition, in his commentary on basketball he had no peer in the entire Mid West.

"Would you care for a walk about town?" Gotz invited me insistently, and plunked his whisky glass down on some quote for industrial gas oil.

"OK." I was not in a position to object, and anyway, the only thing that interested me was to find out what kind of job he meant and how much I was going to earn weekly.

We went out of the building and got in an enormous black Cadillac.

Its interior was equipped with a refrigerator, a bar for drinks, an ice generator, a coffee-machine with a grinder, and something that even then, at the very beginning of the nineties of the twentieth century, I saw for the first time: a cellular telephone exchange mounted inside the car.

"I also have Mercedes and Porsches, but today I am in a patriotic mood. Ha-ha!" Gotz chuckled and drove through the town.

The first site we dropped in at was an azure office building with a beautiful green two-story pizza restaurant. That was just a tiny little pearl in the massive crown of properties of this king. The waiters at the restaurant were Latino boys. They looked upon Gotz and treated him somehow both as a God and also with casual familiarity.

"Look at this one: Jose. I took him from Honduras. My wife and I were having dinner at some restaurant in Tegucigalpa, while he was standing there, dirty and homeless, looking up at us from across the street below. Look at him now!"

Jose grinned, showing clean and perfectly American-like, well cared for, white teeth. He was dressed in new, diligently hemmed, working clothes with the name of the restaurant inscribed on the chest. His hair was gently smoothed with light gel. He radiated servility combined with the behavior of someone just beginning to be overindulged, along with a sugary cleanliness. Right then, at that very moment, watching Gotz's cooks, dishwashers, cleaning boys and waiters, some deep and unpleasant doubt cut me to the quick. I could never find out the truth, but it was strange to me that the memory of that doubt never faded away. It remained in my consciousness forever, transforming my insight from its original form at that moment to the never-answered question "Exactly what did Gotz need those boys for?"

After the restaurant we set out to another business achievement of the millionaire. It was a U-shaped office compound built and arranged truly exquisitely and with style, a low-storied solution which did not impose itself on its surroundings, and which did not oppress or offend the eye with abstract shapes. There was enough breathing place, and the parked cars were lost amid greenery, fountains and cafes. The offices themselves resembled two- and three-storied family homes without any concrete, steel, lead glass or aluminium. Everything was built out of small, warm and beautiful bricks, bright red, combined with very attractive woodwork, colorful vitrages and broken up light slits. The central part of the big U was occupied by a travel agency. Most of the businesses here were Gotz's tenants, but not that agency. It turned out that it was owned by Gotz himself.

Since the working hours were already over and night was drawing near, there was no one in the comfortable office. Ben Gotz showed me the color leaflets of various islands, mountains, seas and lakes from all the five continents, plus Oceania. He demonstrated for me the computer software for booking airplane tickets and luxury cruises. He bragged about his low prices and exotic destinations.

"So, let's get to work now!" He raised his finger.

"He finally remembered to grab the bull by the horns", I said to myself. I was already seriously worrying that he might have forgotten the reason for which he had made me travel that long way from one state to another. I became all ears with tension. I imagined Gotz offering me some terrific, highly paid job. I fantasized how my life would begin to flow, as if in a movie. I had the thrilling feeling that my fate would suddenly change with a headlong flight upwards. I was already beginning to believe in the American dream, forgetting its nightmare.

"Now, look here, young man: your university has, how many? Probably ten thousand students, right?"

"Fifteen thousand."

"Wonderful! Magnificent, even grandiose! So, say at least ten percent of those are foreigners, right?"

"Hm-m, I think they are actually more than two or three thousand, Mr. Gotz."

"OK! Wonderful! Therefore, they travel to their home countries at least twice a year, right? In the summer and around Christmas?"

"Yes, most of them do."

"Where do they come from mainly? Asia?"

"True, most of them are from Asia. But there are also some from Africa, and there are also quite a few from Europe. The number of those from South America is not small either..."

"Aha. So here is the picture: you will be offering them air tickets. You'll stick ads around the university. You'll also tell all your friends. Given my prices, the turnover is guaranteed! I am going to give you ten percent on each ticked sold. This is a very generous offer on my side. In a short time you'll make a pile of money! Is it a deal?"

My soul ached. Ben Gotz had just destroyed all my hopes, and in no time at all. In the first place, the cleaners at the university campus never neglected to rip such ads off the walls and shovel them out of the corridors of the university buildings. In the second place, my vague remembrance of reading those meaningless bits of paper in passing showed that Gotz's prices were at least twenty or thirty percent higher than the rest! And there was a third thing, the most insulting to me: to work for some ephemeral, unproven, uncertain, almost imaginary percentage! From some unmarketable commodity! My hopes for a prestigious job and guaranteed high and stable monthly pay were gone! Instead, I got an indescribably dull offer, insulting in its brainless absurdity!

It could not be helped; we drove back toward Gotz's basic residence and personal office. I had left my car there. His mobile rang while we were on the road. It was his wife. They discussed for a long time what brand and what flavor of ice cream he should buy for "after dinner".

It was time for me to go. I didn't say anything to the baron. Out of courtesy, I took his card and lied that I was going to move on the issue and call him. He stuck in my hands a pile of offers and leaflets, pricelists and deceptive cards for illusory discounts. Well, I had experienced one more futile hope and, as an inevitable consequence, one more disappointment. It was not a bitter one, but a cautionary experience. That was why I was happy that I was leaving. I could no longer breathe the air surrounding Ben Gotz. Meanwhile, he did not stop babbling.

"We, the solid people in this city, have a club of our own, the Noble Club. We are very powerful in every respect."

"Uh-huh." I nodded apathetically.

"And you can rely on us!"

"That sounds interesting, Mr. Gotz."

"We have a great number of charity activities."

"That's good too."

"We have annual campaigns."

"Good for you!"

"You can coordinate the Christmas campaign at your university."

"OK, OK."

"We act together from now on, don't we?"

"By all means."

"That's the spirit! So, a deal, right?"

"A deal."

"See you soon! Drive carefully!"

"Will do, bye!"

"Ah, wait, you're interested in literature, aren't you?"

"That's right."

"See, I nearly forgot to tell you. We have a Poe Society here. You know who he is, don't you? Edgar Allan?"

"I do."

"Well, the Poe Society gathers every year and leaves a bottle of cognac on his grave. Ha-ha-ha! And remember what I told you at the beginning! But now I've decided to modify and additionally specify my own quote. Here is the new version: "He who has come to know the truth, is miserable. That's all! Who cares if he's adamant?"

* * *

Oh, I remembered forever the drive back to Illinois! I remembered the empty, dark and narrow road, the overhanging century-old beeches, through which the pagan moon was copulating occultly on the yellow line with the even more threatening line of my own headlights, surrounded by thick, horrifying darkness. I remembered the artificial light in a world without sun, a road to a chimerical reality, temporary for no one knew how long. An essential part of my young life had become wrapped up in those years in the insoluble hypothesis of a strange interjection, and was suddenly flung away, like the stanzas of a formally arranged narrative poem which, once having been broken up, transposed and scattered aside the stanzas of predestined desire.

When I entered Edwardsville, it was already 10:30 p.m. But even though tired from driving, I did not yet feel like going to my lonely place, especially after the explosion of the Ben Gotz balloon. I decided to drop in on a good colleague and friend of mine, Daniel Ensam Ze. He was the nephew of the President of Cameroon, Ensam Ze. Moreover, he was my neighbor. We lived in the same neighborhood, East College, only his house was several blocks away from mine, an end building by the riverside and the oak forest starting from there. I left the car in the parking lot in front of my dormitory and set out on foot.

He welcomed me familiarly and poured some drinks.

I relaxed. The familiar ritual brought me back to myself. For some unknown reason we mentioned Patrice, a strange person whom one could meet at various places in the city: from student parties to the scrap depot where he worked for four bucks an hour; from the library to the maintenance and cleaning of the latrines; from the demonstrations in front of the First National Bank in support of Leonard Peltier, to the illegal, cheap service stations, where he repaired cars for fifteen bucks a shift...

"Actually, where does Patrice come from?" I asked.

"Oh, he too comes from Cameroon. Like me," Daniel sighed and frowned. "He discredits my country."

"Because he is critically disposed?"

"And not only because of that. Apart from constantly bespattering me and my uncle here, I have no idea where he lives or where exactly he works or what exactly he is doing... A degenerate."

"He often turns up at the student parties. He always pops up uninvited, as if from the bowels of the earth, armed with radical ideas. Sometimes I argue with him; sometimes he makes me ponder seriously. Moreover, he seems to maintain his self-control when he is talking. He never behaves like an irresponsible lumpenprol."

"On the contrary! He's exactly that! He is just a miserable man, yet he pretends he knows the truth."

* * *

When I said goodbye to Daniel and thanked him for the drink and the company, it was already midnight. I walked along the murmuring river toward my home. A light wind was carrying through the darkened old oak trees the songs of Illinois.

Suddenly, I heard a voice from the deep gorge, mingling with the water murmur:

"You were at Daniel Essam Ze's, weren't you? The nephew of that one who sold out Cameroon! First to France, then to England, and look, he has attached himself to America now! But, to hell with him, we will cope with him ourselves one day. But you! You, who want to be like your white brothers and to become Massa! You have to know that they will never accept you as an equal! Never!

I had no doubt at all that it was Patrice's voice.

Oskar Kokoschka, KGB, and FBI

It happened back in 1988 in New York. I was working for the Bulgarian KGB. My diplomatic cover was the Bulgarian Consulate in Manhattan.

I received an unexpected letter from the Bulgarian Foreign Office. Briefly, they were informing me about the forthcoming visit of Mr. Sendoff and his wife. Mr. Sendoff was a world famous mathematician, member of the Bulgarian Academy of Science, and, most importantly in my case – a member of the Parliament. That is why I was saddled with the task of organizing the whole visit of the Sendoffs in New York.

The story I am sharing with you happened in the Museum of Modern Art.

On the way to the Museum, I was observing two big black cars with tinted windshields in my rear mirror. Nothing unusual, I had been accustomed to the company of my "best friends" from FBI for a long time. We had been playing our silent game for years in the streets of New York. My favorite part was the turnpikes. Sometimes a turnpike would give me the chance to lose my tail.

Well, this time I did not play any tricks on FBI. My task was solely diplomatic. I had nothing to hide that day. I was rarely calm and confident. "A smooth day. Feels like a vacation", I thought.

I parked the car in 53rd Street, between Fifth Avenue and Avenue of the Americas. I saw how the two FBI vehicles also stopped and parked just 25 yards behind us.

We entered the Museum. Two FBI officers us in their dark suits were following. They walked silently past our group, through all the halls, through all the exhibitions. At that moment a joyfully ironic thought popped up my mind: "Exhibition is a contradiction in terms."

We entered the hall with the collection of Oskar Kokoschka. Mrs. Sendoff was a big fan of the Austrian painter. In addition, she was participating the managing board of an art foundation. Before I could do anything, she broke all the rules. She pulled out a small camera and she took a picture of Kokoschka's *The Dreaming Boys*. A museum guard approached, I apologized to him, explaining the situation and promised this would not happen again. But that was not what I was worried about. The museum was my slightest problem. My spy consciousness analyzed my senses and immediately told me where the biggest problem was.

When Mrs. Sendoff took the picture of *The Dreaming Boys* I saw two black-suited boys next to the painting. And, guess what, they were not dreaming. They were our silent followers from the FBI. So, she actually took a picture of two FBI undercover officers without any authorization.

Now I literally blushed. And, trust me; I had not been blushing for years before that.

I tried to look for the FBI guys to see their reaction. But they had magically disappeared out of my sight.

"Why did you do this?", I asked Mrs. Sendoff.

"Well, I could not refrain myself. This is one of my favorite paintings in this world.", she said in the most dramatically snobbish voice you could imagine. "Plus, - she continued. - Expressionism does not live in an ivory tower, like Kokoschka himself used to say!"

I was so angry that I managed to confine myself of saying only the following:

"Oh, really? Now I can assure you FBI will not be sitting in an ivory tower, too. Not to mention in what kind of tower I might be sitting soon if they make an official complaint to KGB!"

When we walked out of the museum I was still nervous and cold-sweating.

I opened the car door for Mr. Sendoff. I pretended I am forgetting to open the door for Mrs. Sendoff. She got the message, made a caustic and pretentious face and entered the car herself.

I was just about to open my door. I was pulling the ignition key out of my jacket's pocket when one of the FBI officers approached me.

"Colleague, you are doing your job and we are doing our job. That is why I am convinced you are aware what you did today was wrong!", he said.

I looked scarily at Mr. and Mrs. Sendoff. Luckily, the car windows were all closed so they could not hear anything.

"Colleague, I deeply apologize", I replied. "It won't happen ever again. I will personally take the responsibility and I will destroy the film inside her camera."

He looked at me in disbelief:

"Oh, yeah? And how do we know you did not do all this on purpose?"

I felt really embarrassed. The situation was ridiculous, at the same time it was awkward and unpleasant.

"Listen, guys", I said sincerely, "Nothing was on purpose. Take my word. I am even more pissed off than you are. I am sorry, guys!"

"Ah, okay.", he replied, turned around, made a gesture with his hand meaning "whatever" and walked toward the first of their two big black cars.

They were still angry, I knew it. So was I. Very. And, obviously not with them.

It has been 24 years since then. I live in New York City.

But even now, after so many years, I am very cautious when I see a Kokoschka painting.

And, to tell you the truth, I did manage to take the film out of Mrs. Sendoff's camera. I kept my promise to my American colleagues. But I did not destroy the film. I never passed it to anybody else from Bulgarian KGB. I kept it to myself. I developed the pictures and I put the most special one in a frame. It reminds me of my past as a spy, among many other gadgets: *The Dreaming Boys* by Oskar Kokoschka with two FBI agents on each side.

My New Yorker Love

Tina Dobbs was the fiction editor at *The New Yorker*. She was taller than me, quite slender, with pale cheeks, reddish straight hair and auburn eyes. She was sophisticated, famous, rich, and powerful.

I met her at *The New Yorker* Festival in October 2009. Tina was hosting a meeting with the Pulitzer Prize winner JhumpaLahiri. I spoke in front of the audience in Astor Place Theater and I praised Jhumpa for her books - especially for her first novel *The Namesake*. I shared with the audience how impressed I had been by the movie *The Namesake*. I found the best words and I was expressing my feelings about Lahiri's work and literary achievement warmly.

Now, to tell you the truth, I actually lied. I did not like Lahiri's writing. I did all this just in order to impress Tina Dobbs. And I thought I had impressed her. She thanked me for my positive comments and the audience applauded me. A Chinese immigration lawyer sitting next to me extended her hand, shook mine, and congratulated me for my success. I felt in the seventh heaven.

In the next evening I went to the City Winery. The whole *New Yorker* staff was there. I managed to briefly stop Tina Dobbs in front of the band, just when the event was about to start. I told her I had submitted two short stories to her fiction department and I gave her my business card. She was cold enough, her attitude was rather lukewarm, and she did not give me her business card. At the same time, she promised she would read my stories and would reply to me. Having said this, and looking down at my business card and not in my eyes, she excused herself with the fact that event was starting and she had to return to the others from *The New Yorker* at the stage. The band started playing loudly: "Radar Love..."

And that is how my obsessive radar love with the fiction editor of *The New Yorker* started.

At night, in my small basement room in Upper West Side, I always imagined Tina's lukewarm expression and for some reason I felt even more attracted by her coldness. You could call me a masochist and you could be damned right as well.

I even imagined me in front of her, bent my head and passionately waiting for her only look, for her only smile. Anyway, I felt I had to do something. But what?

I started wandering around Conde Nast building on 42nd Street every single day. I went to the security, they sent me to the mail department and I left my books to be delivered to Tina Dobbs.

My wandering around Conde Nast was useless. I never got the chance to see Tina.

Once I was close. There was a literary event near Lincoln Plaza. I spoke with the head of the security and he allowed me to wait by the door. Apparently, a limo with a nicely dressed driver was waiting for Tina. But guess what – it appeared Tina had left through an auxiliary exit, by another limo, with another driver! And I stood in front of the door two hours for nothing! Yes, she stood me up!

On the next morning I felt I had to do something decisive. I went to Bryant Park, bought a cup of coffee, and I lighted a cigarette. 'Think, think, think!', I was telling myself. 'Please, do not crush me, New York!'

And suddenly, an insight took all over my suffering being. I looked up and I saw the top of Empire State Building through the trees in Bryant Park. Oh, heavens! There the answer was! A park orchestra started playing Beethoven's 9th Symphony. Yes, there was a way!

Meanwhile, that night I got an email by Tina Dobbs. She was rejecting my short stories. Deeply disappointed, I wrote to her:

Dear Mrs. Dobbs,

I am aware of the fact that you are extremely busy.
But is that the only reason for your rejection?

Is this because of some prejudice on the basis of my origin?

Probably in your eyes I am just some Eastern European trash. Even during JhumpaLahiri event, when I spoke, your face expression implied : "Oh, a monkey which actually speaks English!"

I am a well-published writer and I do not feel very well (this is the softest way I could put it) when I am segregated or discriminated on the basis of geographical location or origin. I perceive such an attitude as an extreme intellectual cruelty/violence against me. Segregation of an author on the basis of his/her origin – sounds bad for any institution. Smells like some new kind of racism.

Is everything o.k. with you? Are you angry with me? Have I insulted you unintentionally? If that is the case, I apologize. Still, I do not believe I have said or done anything because of any bad intentions.

The more you keep on rejecting me, the more I feel like Ralph Ellison's Invisible Man. But this time the Invisible Man is not an African-American. This time he is a writer from the former Eastern Europe (now EU), member of his country's Union of Writers and PEN Club. An author who is somewhat famous at home and now lives and writes in America.

I wish you a Merry Christmas (which happens to be my birthday) and a prosperous 2010.

Kind regards,

Steve Nahum

Unexpectedly, her reply came right away:

Mr. Nahum,

The problem here is one of administration, not racism, which would not have occurred to me; your accusations are very far off-base, both offensive and aggressive.

You can imagine that I have literally thousands of people sending manuscripts to me. I am not able to strike up a personal relationship with all of these writers; there simply isn't enough time in the day. But I consider the work fairly and without prejudice.

Sincerely,

Tina Dobbs

There we go! Another lukewarm attitude, no love at all. No love in the hearts of these people who rule *The New Yorker*. No love in those who rule New York. No love in New York. I had to do something. I had to act fast. The insight I received from the heaven above Bryant Part was the answer. I had to follow this remedy suggestion from the skies. It was my salutary road.
I went to the Empire State Building, paid the $30 entrance; I went all the way to the top, exchanging two different elevators, surrounded by tourists from all over the world. I was the only one in this crowd who was here for a quite different reason. I was the distinguished visitor. I was refusing to be humble. I was reacting with energy of a cosmic nature to the rejection.

When I reached the top of Empire State Building I scooted to one of the telescopes there. I inserted a quarter and I pointed the telescope toward Conde Nast building.

And there she was! Quite slender, with pale cheeks, reddish straight hair and auburn eyes.Sitting in her cozy glassy corner office, looking at her computer screen, with her glasses on.The cold Queen of world fiction in her icy palace.

The telescope machine was asking for another coin. I inserted my next quarter and I continued my astronomic activity. Suddenly a tall guy entered her office. For God's sake, this was Johnny the Rock Bear himself. Yes, the rock star. And they kissed!

I stood by my telescope quite a long time, inserting quarter after quarter.

Finally, a lady security officer approached me and said: 'Sir, would you mind stepping away from the telescope, because there are many other tourists here who want to use it.'

'Officer, have you got a spare quarter by chance?', I replied.

'Sir, did you hear what I had just told you?', the security officer was getting nervous on my behavior.

'Yes Madam, I did', I said.

'So please step aside from the telescope!'

'Officer, I am not a tourist'

'It does not matter who you are. Last warning: step aside'

I had to leave my magic view. I had to depart from my Tina.

I stepped away from the telescope and it was immediately occupied by a bunch of Japanese tourists.

'I am sorry, officer', I said.

'There is no need to apologize. So if you are not a tourist what kind of business do you have here?', she asked.

'It is simple, officer. A love business, New York love business. I fell in love with a New Yorker and now I feel bad.'

Security officer shook her head, turned around, and walked back inside the building. I had no more reasons to stand there on the top of the world. My telescope was taken away from me. It was devastating.

It was only after this occurrence when it came to me to check Tina's biography on Internet. I realized she was actually married to Johnny the Rock Bear. I knew nothing about her life. I was seeing myself only.

I sat by my computer and I wrote to Tina:

Dear Tina,

I am writing this time to apologize and to say I am sorry for my behavior. Please disregard all the nonsense, foolish, and imbecile things I said in my e-mail. My feelings were hurt and I let myself be driven by negative emotions. I feel sorry for myself, because what I said does not represent who actually I am and what actually I am as both a writer and a person. The truth is I think you are a very fair and very sophisticated lady. I acted quite stupidly, feeling rejected as an author. On my behalf, I will remember only the positive part of our communication. Once again, please accept my deepest apology.

Sincerely yours,
Steve

And guess what, on the next day an answer came:

Dear Steve,

I appreciate the apology, and I wish you the best of luck with your writing.

Best wishes,

Tina Dobbs

Well, that was it. So much for my New Yorker love. I had to accept the facts.

By the way, my novel got published, I became rich and famous. I moved to a nice apartment in midtown Manhattan. I can see Conde Nast building from my window.

Today I opened the latest issue of *The New Yorker*. I saw an interesting advertisement about telescopes sale. And, guess what! I am going to order one.

The Painting of the Wormy Apple

Way back when I was a young reporter for *The Southern Illinoisan Review*, I was assigned the task to come here to you, New Yorkers, to interview the great Theodor Maier.

Once the boss gave me the order, I didn't dawdle for a second. I jumped into my old reliable Ford, drove fast along the corn fields, and then took the first available flight from Saint Louis.

Somehow like greased lightning, I found myself in Manhattan.

I got an Italian coffee near Times Square and immediately telephoned Maier, who suggested we meet on a corner in Soho.

He met me frowning and led me towards 'The House of Shadows'. It was a combination of a free studio for young talent, a café, and an exhibition hall. He had created it himself with his own funds, and over the years it had turned into a compulsory address for many artists. Here painters, poets, and writers used to mainly drink cocktails called 'Smoke above the Water' with true smoke seen by eyewitnesses and reported as being 'very fragrant, with the flavor of fig'. Actors and singers preferred tall drinks with little umbrellas and ribbons, while, according to other onlookers and art-loafers, the playwrights, script writers, and directors clung to the strange greenish "Rimbaud" cocktail, the taste of which brought to mind a forbidden drink, or maybe in fact it did not just bring to mind, but was true absinthe. Some of the clientele had become popular thanks to 'The House of Shadows', others came to exploit their popularity, while the rest were simply striving for popularity. Well, no doubt, there were bores as well. As for the presence of persons normally defined as 'snobs', that you can guess for yourself. You can even sniff them throughout the text.

That particular evening was not much different. I feasted my eyes on their New York faces, enjoyed the greenish, violet, orange, dark red, crimson, yellow and pink shadows of Soho, which crisscrossed the streets from under the eaves, danced on the broad, varnished boards of the gallery, rustled mysteriously with the whisper of the flattering promise of fame, of New York success, of New York frivolity, of cosmopolitan freedom…

"I don't drink liquor anymore, or did you forget?" Maier scolded the waiter rudely, bringing me out of the trance. "Bring me… mineral water. And a strawberry shake."

"Same for me…" I murmured under my nose.

"Shit! Bring the young man a double whiskey. No objections!"

Only now, I noticed with relief that Maier was capable of smiling. For some unknown reason, this smile brought to my mind someone else's image that was associated in a funny way with the earlier stern and frowning face of the person in front of me, which I vaguely remember having spotted while leafing through old numbers of the New Yorker in preparation for the interview…

I sighed and leaned back. I took out my block note.

"Don't sigh, young man! I already know that this interview is stupid, boring and unnecessary! I only agreed because you don't come from the New York press! You have… H'm…" He looked at his watch. "You have exactly ten minutes."

"But… OK… I…"

"And since ten minutes are awfully few, better forget the questions about my bio, creative impulses, new painting, and padding like that, so you don't waste the sand flowing fast through the invisible, but exact and unyielding hourglass, and thus wind up getting fired from your little magazine! And, by the way, I have no new paintings. I am already seventy years old; you know this. One piece of advice from me: focus on a single thing. It will give you a good small piece that'll make your editor-in-chief happy, ha-ha! I have just hinted at it. What is it?"

"A-a-h… Maybe… That I don't come from a New York magazine?"

"Correct! So far, I like you. And unless you interrupt me and ruin your own job, and if you keep silent, take notes, and then go quietly back to the corn fields of the Midwest, then at least one night I won't curse American journalism! How about that, is it a deal?"

"Absolutely."

"Very good." Maier sipped from his water, without touching the shake. "The New York press sang my praises, called me the new El Greco. 'The Manhattan Monumentalist', 'The Philosopher of Soho', 'The Titan of the Eastern Coast'.

"This, Mr. Maier, has probably to do with…"

"Yes, it does. Why are you interrupting me?"

"I'm specifying in order to help the readers of *The Southern Illinoisan Review*."

"You'll specify later, when you edit your text! OK?"

"Understood."

"So. It has to do, as you dared to guess, with the fact that I'm one of the founders of that movement, which at the time named New York 'The Big Apple'. In that connection, the press kept blaring forth about me: 'An American Classic', "An Integral Commander of Colors', 'A Master of the Profound Context', 'A Fine Aesthete', 'A Perfect Unifier of Color and Message', 'The Admiral of the New York Artist Fleet'. Even Michael Krantz was forced to capitulate."

"Who is Michael Krantz?"

"Young man, you are forgiven that you don't know much about art. But even the marshals in Southern Illinois should have heard of him."

"But why the marshals?"

"Because Michael Krantz is the worst enemy of New York. He's the author of a contemporary military dictatorship much more awful than that of Hitler or Stalin!

"But what is he?"

"A critic, of course. A tyrannical and powerful critic. A legislator and an executioner at the same time."

At that moment, something in Maier's face had turned gloomy again, which startled and amazed me. I sensed a euphoric mixture of a constrained 'Eureka!' cry; a voice that was drumming inside my poor, inexperienced and green for the New York life head, and a matter-of-fact hand slapping me on the neck: 'For God sake, don't speak and even don't breath!' For I suddenly saw Michael Krantz. Yes, I had read an article about him. An article with… a photo of the man. There was some weird likeness, no, rather a visible semblance. An unwished for and uncomfortable likeness imposed by Mother Nature, a boring fact disputed and obviously denied by both of them. So… that was it! For me, the greenhorn from Southern Illinois, it was a discovery, but for New York it had been a long existing and very spicy tidbit of a public secret. And exactly one of those town whispers that tastes most sweet on the tip of the tongue and makes life in the Big Apple worthwhile.

"Whereas the two of you…"

"Whereas the two of us did not like each other very much at all… Now we are both getting old and people are beginning to forget us…" Maier sighed. "But, back to the topic! So. At one point a new inspiration came upon me and I painted 'The Wormy Apple'."

"A very famous painting. It represents 'The Big Apple' with various worms and caterpillars with human faces protruding from it."

"Oh, unexpected flatterer, I know it's famous. Even more, I know what it represents, damn it! But that's not important in this case. Listen now. When I showed it for the first time, everyone was amazed. The New York press carried me towards new horizons and heights: 'A Large-Scale

Legislator', 'A Creator of Eternal Forms', 'An Author of Categories', 'A Founder of a School of His Own'. And so on and so forth, without end. Until a bad moment arrived."

"Probably, just a crucial moment?"

"No, young man, not crucial, just bad and unpleasant. Since then I have stopped talking with the New York press, as I told you at the beginning."

"What happened?"

"Michael Krantz wrote a special article on the painting. He attacked me. And since he didn't have anything else to harass me about, he made something up: that the painting depicted my artist colleagues, with whom I had created the idea of the 'Big Apple'! That I had gotten too big for my britches and made up my mind to cut myself off from them. To denounce them as 'a misbegotten anachronism'. So that's why I had 'put their faces on a rotten fruit of my own dirty sub consciousness". Can you imagine? What meanness on his part! A real scoundrel! An intriguer!"

"While you, in fact…"

"I know what you're going to ask about! No, I didn't have any idea of the kind! All of it was Krantz's lousy plan and mean plot! He wrote that, through the 'Wormy Apple', I had wanted to destroy all the artists of New York so I could stand alone, ensuring for myself a guaranteed and preserved place in the history of our generation! It was completely absurd, but unfortunately people believed him. Many of my dear friends and colleagues took offense, some of them for good. The press followed his lead and began to fire intense fusillades at me from terrific forty-inch cannons: 'An Apologist of the Hypocritical Historical Approach', 'A Stubborn Megalomaniac', 'The Dinosaur of Painting', 'A Speculative Doctrinaire', 'A Conquistador against Thought', 'A Prehistoric Vanguard Artist', 'A Conservative Dogmatist', 'A Retrograde Traditionalist', 'A Focus of Anachronisms', 'An Attempt at Classicism Failed due to a Failure of the Ages to Meet', 'An Anti-Modern Renegade', 'A Servant to Bourgeois Dogma', 'The Anteroom to a Dull Ocean'…"

"Mr. Maier, I really am …"

"You are really sorry?"

"Yes."

"Don't be. That's what press is like. It's called that because it presses you." Maier had gone red and looked harassed. "Well, I think we're done. You have time to ask one last question, if you want. Of course, it is not obligatory."

"My last question is: When you look back, and be absolutely honest, please, did you really have no one in mind when you painted 'The Wormy Apple'?"

"H'm… What can I tell you, young man… For many years now, I've been convinced that I had nobody in mind as I worked. But… Time has proved otherwise. I've dug long and deep and put myself through self-examination. I've discovered the answer. I'll tell you the truth."

I kept silent, waiting anxiously, afraid to utter a sound. Maier groaned, sighed deeply, bent over the table towards me and whispered:

"Yes, it turned out that while I had been painting, the intelligible creativity in me, making the image of the fattest worm poking out of the apple, I had been seeing Michael Krantz's ugly mug."

I kept it all to myself. When I returned to Illinois, I told the boss that Maier had refused to meet with me, and that I had not managed to get an interview. I was immediately fired from *The Southern Illinoisan Review*, an event to which I attribute all my later success as a writer. Theodor Maier died fifteen years ago, but I dare to tell you this story only now, my dear New Yorkers, because I saw Michael Krantz's obituary in The Times just the other day, and I felt free from all constraints regarding that story. You see, dear reader, I came to learn from that "non interview" that within all great artists lies the hidden self critic, an arguing twin, if you will, while within the critic, is the hidden artist, dreaming of the limelight. And, come to think, isn't that true also about all man's activities globally? But in the case that I now call *The Wormy Apple*, my article would have destroyed both men. That might have brought me a certain amount of celebrity at the time, which at that tender age might have obscured the man, indeed the writer I so hoped to become... We have to look in the mirror, once in a while, and often wonder just who is really looking back at us, if not over the shoulder.

The Spring

I am the grass. I am the trees. I am the bushes. The leaves. The saps. They slap me in the face – they want me – believe – breathe through me – forever alive – admittedly.

I run. And I search. I search, and run.

Water is down. The wombs. It springs. It vaporizes. It rains. It soaks up. In the wombs.

Where is the Virginity?

The forest path is real. The vault of heaven is green. Dusk. Brain expansion. Making out, Contemplation, Who understands that, comes back through the time. Purifies himself.

I was said correctly – do not search. Do not search for Him. You cannot find Him.

"To find means to search" – obviously I replied in a meaningless way.

Then I shouted out:

"I am searching for the Virginity! You wasted Her! Where is she? Why? When? When did you make it?"

The peasants turned around mockingly and assured me the spring did not exist.

They are lying. It cannot be so. It is somewhere. It is in that forest. It is what the tear is – submission for harmony. It is the base – before the conception.

The jacket remains on the thorns. The shoes remain on the mud. The trousers destroy themselves mutually with the rocks. A substance and an anti-substance. The body founders on the abysses. The thought dies away in a smashed skull. The spirit kills itself and opens into the outer space. The feelings creep among the blades of grass. They scent out. They desire.

I always imagine him – He will be under a wilding pear tree, all over hedged in blackberry bushes and weeds from hell, He will be perfectly round, perfectly smooth, perfectly clean, cold like a tail of a comet, alive and veracious – He is immortal and has neither for a while had a thought of a lie. He will be untouched, not loved, undrunk from, unseen, imperceptible even by intuition. He will be the first one that only I see, nevertheless if I deserve it, so the Substance will hold in store.

I will lean down and carve my lips into the water resistance. And then I will feel the scent of the worm who eats soil. And of the bacteria who finish off the carrion. And of the stems that drink minerals. And of the drop that chases the Nucleus of one Planet. And then I will suck up. And then I will absorb. Much, Boundlessly, Intangibly, Endlessly. FREELY.

And then… Then I will be Nature. Then I will become Conception. And then – Virginity. I will be before everybody and everything – in a reverse order. Even before the Chaos. Maybe I will even not be.

And presently… Presently I search. Every day. They do not consider me mad – because they despise me. They are beside the Spring. They hate it. They haven't been even in the Stream after the Spring for a long time. Neither in the Sea. They are on Dry Land – there they ruined themselves. There they dressed in Science. There they lost the Feeling. There even the memory of the Spring died. There they decided they are happy.

Before… Before the Purity was. Of yore. Before we were Springs. Before we were grass, trees, bushes, leaves, saps. Before there was a truth.

I am alone against the Entity. Certainly it must be so. According to the Substance, maybe. I do not know – but I am setting for searching the spring which I was said about it was an abstraction.

The Unicorn in Captivity

It was New Year's Eve.

The last visitors were already filing out of the castle. The sun, having long ago rounded Manhattan, was shining its last winter rays on the brownish, snowless hills above the Hudson River, the occasional steep cliffs topped by bare trees. A tall man in a black overcoat and a shawl in the same color, with short, lank hair and large, light brown, slightly moist eyes, climbed up the curving walk, almost running up the stone steps, to buy a ticket before slipping into the museum and vanishing from the view of the guards who lurked behind their favourite backyard flower garden with its small but lovely heptagonal fountain.

The cashier in a dark blue uniform explained to the belated visitor that he had half an hour left, and then he busied himself with the departure of a noisy group of German tourists, who were disappointed, not for the first time, at not being allowed to use their large, long-lens cameras. The cashier and the few guards on duty were happy with the setting in of the holiday: they would have fun with their families, only glancing now and then at the TV broadcasting the raging, drunken crowd on Times Square. They were also equally delighted with the fact that they worked at The Cloisters, the pride of New Yorkers, wherein through various known and unknown ways, some of the best works of art of pre-Renaissance Europe—the forbearer of that terrible Europe of the first half of the twentieth century dealing primarily in settling the demographic problems through reducing the number of her population and nonchalant of her own treasures—had been gathered.

The new visitor, the last one of the day and the year, quickly crossed the greater part of the museum, looking around with an unforced professionalism, even somewhat apathetically, at the paintings, the stained glass, the sculptures, the wonderful figures covered with gold, silver, precious stones, ivory and enamel, until he stopped in one of the midway halls, smaller than the rest, and more scantily illuminated by the artificial light. Here were finely and elaborately crafted tapestries which had arrived in New York by strange whims of both fate and time from cool medieval European castles. The man walked slowly through the hall, then stopped in front of a narrow rectangular tapestry hung on the left wall, just before a middling passage, due to its location, giving the impression of being hung in a slightly darker and more mysterious place, separated from the rest of the museum. It was an antique French tapestry, depicting a white unicorn rearing and waving its tail, its travel hindered on all sides by a small, round, wooden fence. All of this was in a lush little clearing strewn with any number of various flowers, while the unicorn itself was situated under a tall, slender tree of an outlandish genus. Entitled *The Unicorn in Captivity*, the tapestry was in fact a source of pride of the museum, along with several other pieces from the same series. The newly arrived visitor stepped closer to it, peered at the unicorn, the fence, and the little clearing, then stepped back about two yards. Only then did he untie the shawl, take off his dark overcoat, lay it on the floor and sit down lightly without taking his eyes off the image. The guard in this hall was a woman, the only one at the museum, who approached from her corner and said in a smooth, yet strict tone:

"Sir, sitting on the floor is not allowed."

He was quiet for a few seconds then replied without looking at her.

"Madam, I have to inform you that I frankly intend to spend the night right here."

Initially, his French accent made her decide that he was from Louisiana, but the complex sentence caused her to hesitate about that conclusion: perhaps he was indeed from Europe.

"Sir, there are twenty minutes left before closing time."

This time he looked at her and began to speak hurriedly.

"Look, Madam, this is important to me. Some of the most famous tapestries of the unicorn series are kept here in your museum. And, as far as I am concerned, this particular one is the best, the masterpiece of its time. Look at this little clearing with strange flowers. What kind of flowers are they? There aren't such in Europe. And this tree, odd and unreal, as well as the little fence itself, and the unicorn... where do they come from? Can you see how everything is familiar from outside, but when we look closely at the image, we realize that we have never seen anything like it? It is sweet—perfect— and yet its enchanting perfection borders on quiet nightmare. This item in front of us is a metaphysical space created by the slow ease of time through the Middle Ages and continuing on to the very zenith of the Renaissance. Ah, it is like those old French tales, full of fairies, magic cloaks, talking animals, strange castles hidden deep in impassable dens, sad princes, spellbound princesses and enticing, long and telling moans of hunters' horns. This space lives its own conscious life. Each blade of grass in it, each little flower in front of your eyes, develops and improves, preserving its primary harmony. But when does it take place? Why, when unicorns existed too..." His large light-brown eyes became slightly moist. "You know, this is my life... I have several paintings from which I breathe, drink, and take sustenance. Only a few, indeed... Many years ago I couldn't sleep—they would keep haunting me in my sleep, sometimes in my waking too, and would torture me, torment me for a long time, before I realized that I needed them. I was in need of their presence..."

"What's your occupation, sir?" the young, serious woman guard dressed in a blue guard's uniform, interrupted, looking attentively, yet a little mockingly, at him. To her all that, naturally, was groundless, useless hooey. Had this been taking place somewhere in the Midwest, she might have easily taken him for a run-of-the-mill lunatic. However, the fact that she lived in New York and had seen what not in the subway and in the streets, made her just be unimpressed, refrain from jumping to conclusions, and mainly, not show surprise.

"Years ago," he often used this phrase, obviously signifying with it some important, gone forever period in his life, "I was teaching aesthetics at a university in Paris. Yes, Madam, I really labored hard then, preparing myself for every lecture, you know…" He turned back and looked at the unicorn.

"Why did you say "I was teaching"? Do you have another job now?"

"No, Madam, I have absolutely no job whatsoever, except… Years ago I desired to accumulate knowledge and I read hundreds and hundreds of books—I can easily say thousands—to achieve that purpose: to know art perfectly, every single particle of it, every process, method and school. I dealt particularly with visual art, keen on not overlooking any single artist that had ever been born, or any single nameless painting, or any single school. What is more, I was interested in the entire process, down to the very last fiber and technique. I was keen to know how each wonderful result was achieved. And…" His eyes ran quickly all over the place. "And that's exactly where I became completely confused, Madam. Everything was unclear, entangled and invisible, while earlier it had been so orderly and arranged…"

He uttered a short moan resembling a sob and continued.

"After all, what I believed in, what I was gathering—bit by bit—and what I considered symbolic of my own advancement and improvement, collapsed in a millisecond, disappeared, melted away. Most importantly, I didn't need it anymore. I realized that it was simply an absurdity, a definite mistake, loss and nothing more, nothing to be afraid of…" His eyes became troubled again, and he shivered slightly. "Right then the painting had begun to appear to me and I was in a very difficult situation. I left my job. I had no funds. I moved to the countryside and worked as a cleaner and cashier at a movie house. I didn't even want to think of Paris, of the university where I had been teaching. Most detestable and repulsive to me seemed to be my job there, that lie to my own self in the first place, that estrangement from art. I preferred to give up the ghost, preferring to starve rather than go back. I was a maximalist, I wanted to come to know the anatomy of absolute art, and I ended up reaching absolute nothingness, an empty void. But that didn't bring me comfort because I had come full circle, right back to the beginning, although I remained convinced that it was the right way… There, in the museum of that small provincial town, I discovered by mere chance one of my paintings, and in my free time I would go to delight in it.

Meanwhile, an elderly uncle, who was a comparatively wealthy owner of hairdressing shops, passed away and left me an inheritance, which, if meted out frugally, would last me until the end… So I set out around the world following my paintings, since they alone gave me life.

It may seem unbelievable to you, Madam, but I hear lectures when I am watching them. Some living images are whispering to me about nature, about the people and the creatures, and sometimes even about the Cosmos itself, about the Creation, or simply about quite ordinary things. However, everything is so genuine, real, and unexaggerated that I sit as if spellbound and listen, listen for all I am worth…"

"But this is a tapestry, not a painting!" the woman guard exclaimed.

"No, Madam, this too is a painting, yet much finer than many painted in oil. You know, this distinction is alien to me now. When I feel the living image speak to me, I say to myself, 'this is one of my paintings,' and that's that. What does my body matter? Is it my physical body you are talking with now? Madam, I have truly been educated by these living images, and in reply to you, I can only tell you what they told me: *"Art is above cognition thereof."* And the more time I am in their presence, the more truths come like this, right into my head, and that, Madam, is the beauty of it!"

"But you can't spend the night here! Any moment the cashier will come with the guards for a final check, and that's the end of it. Besides, wouldn't you like to celebrate the New Year, like everyone else?" She felt as if she were trying to persuade a small child.

At that moment, the cashier did appear, alone, and looked questioningly at the Frenchman.

"Are you all right, sir?"

"Yes, yes, of course, we've just been having a little chat…"

"He wants to spend the night here," the woman guard said derisively, turning to the cashier to exchange a understanding look.

"Sir, Cloisters is already closed," the cashier announced solemnly and insistently. "I would recommend that you observe the rules, and I wish you a happy holiday," he added in a matter-of-fact tone.

"My best New Year's will be spent here!" exclaimed the man with the moist eyes.

"I am sorry, sir, but that is impossible," the cashier said firmly.

Three guards appeared behind him.

The Frenchman rose slightly, peered feverishly at the cashier and said, "Haven't you ever suddenly felt that you don't know anything, sir? That you don't know even the tiniest bit about the world, and that what you have considered your own knowledge is somewhat strange, foisted upon you, and, what is most important, counterfeit?"

The cashier nodded in the direction of the guards without saying a word.

The man understood.

He stood up, took his overcoat, and dragged his feet towards the exit of the hall, the guards following at a close distance.

Before actually going out, he halted, turned to the unicorn, stared at it. His eyes became even moister and he said quite quietly: "I will, nevertheless, spend the night here, with you. What a merry feast it will be, won't it?! Nobody can ever break our spiritual connection. You are in my heart. Your art has changed me forever."

Then he started towards the stairs.

The cashier and the guards remained for a little while longer, watching through the large windows to see in which direction the strange visitor was headed, just in case he tried to return. It was already past five. The sun had set behind the Hudson, and the park outside was sinking into glimmering twilight. The strange man was striding straight ahead, without looking around. Once he passed the Maple Leaf restaurant, there was no doubt that he was leaving. Now he was ambling along the lane where old Russian emigrants liked to stroll on Sundays, under two large, bare trees, where suddenly, startled by something unseen, two owls flew past, one after another. And this picture remained, became imprinted on the consciousness of the watchers, because it seemed to be somehow living, somehow talking to itself, and telling an unbelievable, yet perfectly real, painfully real, story.

ABOUT THE AUTHOR

Svet DiNahum was born in 1970 in Sofia, Bulgaria, and is of Jewish ancestry. He is a graduate of the Department of Philosophy at Southern Illinois University and currently lives in New York City, Sofia, Vienna, and Frankfurt. He has published short stories in numerous literary magazines in Bulgaria and throughout Europe; his work has been translated into English, German, Russian, Serbian, Turkish, Spanish, and French. His fiction has appeared in US literary magazines such as *Drunken Boat, Gloom Cupboard, Danse Macabre,* and *Audience.* DiNahum is the author of *The Wolf's Howl* (Short Novel, 1994); *The Unicorn in Captivity* (Collection of Short Stories, 2007), RAPTUS (Novel, 2009) *Nicola Against Nicola* (Short Novel & Screenplay, 2012), *The Doctrinaire* (Novel, 2015), and *The Hangman and the Clown* (Stage Play, 2017). *RAPTUS* was a nominee for the Elias Canetti National Literary Award and was subsequently published in the United States by Hammer & Anvil Books (Las Vegas, 2013). Di Nahum serves as Press Secretary for PEN Center Bulgaria, defending human rights and freedom of expression.

Winner of Essay Competition for World Noble Peace Prize Laureates 2013 in Warsaw (and Lech Walesa Foundation) with his essay *Solidarity Restarted.*

Author of screenplays: *The Second Life of Michael Jackson* (2011), *The Unicorn In Captivity* (2012), *Rays* (2013).

In 2012 wins BTV competition for sitcom episode (TV comedy series *Home Arrest*).

Author's website: www.svetdinahum.com

Contact: sdnahum@gmail.com

To the readers in the USA:

Dear American friends,

For writing the truth about the Russian occupation of Crimea, I've been persecuted and harassed in Bulgaria by organizations that are defending the interests of Putin's regime in the Kremlin. I've been targeted by a campaign aimed at discrediting me. I've also been threatened—indirectly — with so-called 'friendly advice' - a Bulgarian Union of Writers member told me personally after the book launch: "You be careful. You are making a provocation. They are organizing things so you'll be defeated." Then, referring to the nerve agent used against a former Russian military intelligence officer who defected to Britain, that same "friend" warned me: "You might eat Novichok just like Sergei Skripal."

But I am walking on the path of truth and I have passed the line of fear. I'm not going to give in.

Svetoslav Nahum, Author, *Escape from Crimea*

Photographs by Natalia Zhurminskaya

КОРТЕЖ
ГЕТЬ!
СХІД
ЗАХІД
РАЗОМ!